Murder in Sonora

A Young Adult Suspense Novel

Lucy M. Dobkins and Terrell Dobkins

Copyright © 2022 by Lucy M. Dobkins and Terrell Dobkins

This is a work of fiction. Names, characters, business, events and incidents are the products of the author's imagination. Any resemblance to actual persons, living or dead, or actual events is purely coincidental

All rights reserved.

Cover Photo by Stephen Musser

For Kassie Anne, Kami, David and
Dalan, and for Elmer

This manuscript was written by my mother, Lucy M. Dobkins in approximately 1990. To my knowledge, it was never submitted to a publisher. I discovered the manuscript in January of 2022 as I was sorting through a box of family memorabilia. My mother passed away in 2009 at the age of 78, after a 7 year struggle with Alzheimers. In her honor, I am completing the process of publishing this wonderfully written young adult suspense novel. The plot of the novel takes place in the small fishing and vacation village of San Carlos, Sonora, Mexico. Our family began traveling to San Carlos in 1962 and for the next 12 years, this was our family Christmas. It became a dear treasure for our entire family, but especially to Mom and Dad. The novel is purely fictional but accurately portrays the beaches, seashore, geology and the mountain, called Tetas de Cabra, overlooking San Carlos.

Lucy was raised in a hardworking farming family in Albuquerque, New Mexico. She graduated from college at New Mexico State University. In her senior year, she was selected as Homecoming Queen. After college, she married Hal L. Dobkins and both were long time educators in Albuquerque. In addition to her career as a teacher and counselor, she was a fashion model and a business owner. She wrote two books that were published in the 1990's. She also has several of her poems published and preserved in the Library of Congress. In all ways, she was a remarkable woman and her memory has been passed down fondly through three generations.

I hope you enjoy her story as much as I enjoyed bringing it to light.

Terrell Dobkins

MURDER IN SONORA

Table of Contents

Chapter 1.

Sleek black vultures, their dark eyes glittering, drifted in slow circles over the marina and watched the scene their senses knew was watery death.

American tourists, appalled, fascinated, hypnotized, crowded around the policemen on the pier.

A chunky officer in the tan uniform of the Guaymas Police kneeled on the splintered planks of the dock and leaned over the edge, reaching. Gently, the incoming tide lapped at the pilings and ever so slowly eased an unrecognizable bundle of trash closer to him.

Perspiration formed on the policeman's forehead and ran in wet streams into the creases of his eyes and down his tense jaws. Irritable with the depressing job and the intolerable heat, he swiped at the sweat with his sleeve. Dark, wet circles edged with salt stained his underarms.

The police officer, grasping the long wooden handle of his grappling hook, tried another time to snag the bundle of soaked, rotting flotsam shaped vaguely like a human body. It drifted back and forth with the current, bumped into a rotting wooden dinghy, rolled, floated away, drifted back again.

One more attempt. The officer set the hook in the shredded, faded rags and grunted. Finally! He had it! He eased the bundle closer, trying not to rip the fiber. Or the flesh.

Other policemen kneeled on the edge of the dock, reached into the chilly water, and lifted a puffy, pasty body onto the dock.

The tourists pushed forward, stared at the horrible corpse, and gasped in revulsion.

"A woman. Young. Seventeen, eighteen. Dark hair. Could be an American," the officer said over his shoulder to the Guaymas Chief of Police. "Can't tell about her eyes; looks like sea creatures must have been nibbling on them. Big hole in the side of her head, too. Don't know how she could have gotten bashed up that bad. Not even if she fell overboard from a boat."

Chief Salinas crouched over the body.

Who was the woman? Was someone missing from Guaymas or San Carlos, or had the tide carried her from someplace down the coast? How had her head gotten crushed? How long had she been dead?

The chief sighed. Why a death now, right at the beginning of the sailfish season when all the tourists would be arriving? Why in a peaceful resort like San Carlos? They'd never had any crime here and that was the way he wanted it. Keep it safe. Keep the torte-Americanos coming. Let them have their vacations on safe, white beaches in Mexico, far away from their congested cities filled with drugs, danger and death. Let them bring their dollars south.

"Wrap her up and take her to the coroner. We can't do anything more 'til we get his report," the chief ordered.

He turned to push his way to the green and white police car and the ambulance, and observed the expressions of horror and fear on the faces of the vacationers. Some of them looked as though they were going to be sick. Why did people always crowd around tragedies if they couldn't stand what they were going to see? He'd never understand human nature, he guessed.

The chief did not notice the man with the slight smile on his face. Secretly satisfied, the man reluctantly turned from the corpse and strolled up the sandy road past the chapel toward the cool, breezy cantina on the beach.

"Your usual?" the barman asked.

"Yeah. Tequila with lime. Make it a double. Real fine morning out there today."

Chapter 2.

"Dad, are you sure you don't want me to leave while you meet with Bill and Eric?" I asked.

"Course not. You need to be learning about my businesses. They're going to be yours one of these days. And anyway, I want you here for another reason, too," my father said.

There was a light knock on the door. Dad's executive secretary, Millie, her hand on the doorknob, smiled. "Senator, Bill and Eric are here to see you."

"Come on in, boys," Dad bawled exuberantly to the men Millie motioned forward. "It's good to see you. You know my daughter Velvet. You know her especially well," he repeated for Bill, a sparkle in his eyes. We had announced our engagement a couple of weeks ago.

"Hi, Bill. Hi, Eric," I said. "Eric, how nice to see you after all these months. Have you been making my dad rich?"

"No, it's the other way around," Eric grinned and gave me a big hug. "You're looking good, Velvet. Washington must agree with you. Is it Washington's political climate as opposed to the Dallas climate?"

"Well, they can both be hot and windy," I laughed. "Of course, Bill and I will probably live here after we marry. Bill grew up on a northern Minnesota farm and I grew up on a south Texas ranch. We figure it can't get any colder or any hotter than those places and Washington's a good compromise."

My father motioned us into chairs in front of his massive, cherry-wood desk and strode energetically to the other side. He settled himself in his worn and comfortable leather executive chair, crossed his arms over his chest, leaned back, and regarded us thoughtfully.

Eric's eyes swept the office—the impressive desk, brown leather sofa and armchairs and brass coffee tables, deep carpeting and large picture windows overlooking the capitol.

"There's quite a contrast between this handsome office and your modest senate office a few blocks away," Eric commented.

Dad grinned. "Sure is. The senate office keeps me dedicated and humble. This one keeps me scrambling to make a living."

I've just turned eighteen and I'm about to gain access to the trust fund Dad and Mother set up for me when I was little. Dad wants me to learn about his businesses, and I'm sure he hopes I'll take them over some day. Recently when he was talking to me about his oil fields, he said, "You might say I'm financially substantial," but confidentially, I think the actual translation is that he's a multimillionaire. He'd never say so outright, though.

Other people do seem to consider him to be fairly well off. But he's earned everything he has. Dad has spent his entire lifetime working on cattle ranches, in feed lots and oil fields, and in Dallas and Houston real estate.

A few days ago Dad was going over some business with me and said that even after the recent recession he could still afford this new oil field Eric was negotiating to buy. I've noticed Dad's not about to give up his other business activities, or our house in the Maryland woods, either.

Besides his involvement in various businesses, my father is also a U. S. Senator. Senator Stephan J. Shepard of Texas. Dad is well over six feet tall, and he's thin and muscle-hard from ranching. He's as much at ease in Levis and flannels as he is in the suits that are custom-tailored for him in Washington. His hair is silver, but it's still thick and wavy.

Mother used to tell me that when she met my father he was short on money but had all the good looks in the world, and the older he got and the harder he worked, the more he had of both.

There are creases in Dad's face now, of course, and they seem incongruent with his high energy levels; he has the spirit and vigor of a man of forty-five, not sixty-five. I don't want to brag, but I think he's very distinguished looking. Of course, I am prejudiced.

Dad regarded Eric and Bill with respect, but also with affection. Eric Swanson, tall and broad across the shoulders, tan, freckled, his hair bleached from working outdoors in the Southwest oil fields, is Dad' broker. "A damn good one, too," Dad says. I think it's partly because Eric is so good-natured and kind to everyone.

My fiancé Bill Morgan is one of Dad's in-house attorneys. That's how we met. Right here in Dad's office.

"He's brilliant, intense and ambitious, and no detail is too small to capture his attention," Dad says. "That's part of what makes him so valuable."

He's also handsome. Not the rugged, rough-cut handsomeness you see in the movies these days, though he has more of a clean, clear-eyed, well-groomed Philadelphia look. Or San Francisco, maybe. You know, intelligent and alert.

"Bill, is the contract for this deal ready to sign?" Dad asked. "We have a meeting set for three o'clock this afternoon."

"Yes, sir," Bill answered. "The papers are in order. It's a good contract for all parties; everybody will benefit from the terms." He handed a file of documents across the desk to Dad.

"Good. I'll study them before we meet. I want you to be here."

He directed his attention to Eric. "You probably would like to know when you'll get your commission."

Eric nodded. "Yes, sir."

"My secretary will hand-carry the contract to the comptroller first thing tomorrow, and your check should be ready by Wednesday. Do you want us to mail it to your office in Denver, or do you want to pick it up here?"

"Thank you, sir," Eric said. "As a matter of fact, I plan to stay in Washington for a few days—I have some people to see—so I can drop by and pick it up." He grinned sheepishly. "I'll sort of enjoy the weight of it in my pocket."

I just happened to know that the check would be in the range of $270,000. I'd want to carry it in my pocket, too, if I had the chance.

"Fine. Do that," my father said.

Eric and Bill stood to shake Dad's hand and leave.

"Hold on, both of you. Just because you're young and in a hurry doesn't mean you can't sit a minute and chew the fat, does it?"

The men sat down.

Chapter 3.

"Eric, you probably didn't know it before today, but as you've just found out, Bill here has gotten himself engaged to Velvet. They don't plan to get married 'til Velvet graduates from Georgetown University two years from now. Political science. Still wants to be somebody's campaign manager, although after watching me all these years, I can't imagine why." Dad looked at me as though I had a cog missing.

Eric extended his hand to Bill. "Congratulations. You'll be good for each other."

"It may be good for them," Dad said, "but it's a problem for me. Bill says one Shepard at a time is all he can handle, so he's given me his resignation effective June first. For the life of me, I can't figure out why he chose Velvet over me. This girl's a cross between a petunia and a barbed wire fence."

"Oh, Dad..." I objected.

I knew this was not the first time Dad had protested Bill's resignation, but we all knew it was the right thing to do.

"I'm joining the law firm of Morgan, Mitchel and Pierce," Bill said. "Before Velvet and I get married, I hope to have my practice established. She wants a career, too, and I don't have any problem with that. We can build together."

I nodded. We had lots of plans for our future.

Dad said to Eric, "You haven't seen Velvet since her mother's funeral last winter, have you?"

"No, I haven't. How's she doing?"

They were talking about me as though I had left the room. It was like watching a home movie.

"Aw, who can tell?" Dad said with a shrug. "The frantic pace she keeps, you'd think she's trying live her whole lifetime all at once. She's always studying or working or on the go, full of energy and laughter, surrounded by friends. But then, out of the clear blue, she'll turn quiet and moody, and her eyes will fill with tears. I think she misses her mother more than any of us know."

It was true. But how can you explain to anybody how deep the emptiness is?

For a moment the room was silent. My father was lost in his own unspoken memories, his face terribly sad. I wanted to hug him. Or cry for him.

"I want to get my daughter out of town, away from the rat-race, and I want to do another deal," Dad said.

Eric and Bill raised their eyebrows in surprise. I could see the wheels turning in their minds. Another deal already? Had Dad found an oil field himself? Had he negotiated for it on his own? He was certainly capable of it, but when did he have the time?

"Eric, you're a scuba diver," Dad said. "You've dived in some pretty exotic locations. We're all fascinated by your adventures, and we want to learn to dive, but I can't take the time right now."

Eric was curious. What was the senator planning this time?

"My proposal is this," Dad began to reveal.

"We have a beach house in Mexico on one of the best scuba diving bays in the world. We have a cook and a gardener who look after the house and yard. There's a little fishing dinghy on our private beach, and a nice twenty-one-and-a-half-foot boat moored at the yacht club."

Eric and Bill and I listened. What in the world did Dad have in mind?

"I want you to take any friends you want and go down to our house early in June, if you can arrange it, and teach Velvet and Bill to dive. You'll provide all the scuba gear and wet suits—I'll reimburse you, of course—and you'll use our boats. What do you think?"

Eric's grin provided the answer. "That would be terrific! I'd love to teach them, and I sure would enjoy the use of your house and boats. And cook. And gardener."

"All right. That's set. You all get out of here now and let me get on to the next thing. Go have lunch on me, and make your plans. If you need me to do anything, Velvet can let me know."

He stood, shook hands with his attorney and broker, and handed me a couple of folded bills. Lunch money.

Just like when I was a little kid. On a Washington scale, now, though.

"Thanks, Dad!" I exclaimed and hugged his neck. "This will be a summer I'll never, ever forget!"

Little did I know...

Chapter 4.

Bill, Eric and I left Dad's office and said goodbye to Millie, his secretary. We walked briskly four blocks up the avenue to The Clambake. I figured we might as well begin eating seafood today and get into the spirit of the ocean.

"Well, when do you want to start?" Eric asked in the restaurant that looked like an old oak and brass sailing ship. There were antique lanterns, coils of rope, and anchors with barnacles encrusted on them.

"My last exams will be on May twenty-first," I said. "Why don't I fly to San Carlos as soon as they're finished? That will give our housekeeper-cook Maria and me time to open the house and fill the refrigerator. Bill, can you fly down when your vacation starts on the first of June?"

"Yes, probably," he nodded.

"Eric, do you know who you want to bring?"

"Yes, a good friend who is also a diver, Penny Allen. She can help you learn to dive. And I'd like to ask a couple of kids who were with us on a trip to China last summer, Jade Sando and Lee Long. Lee is from Shanghai, but he's in Denver this year, living with Jade's family and attending Colorado University."

"That's interesting," I said. "Why is he doing that? Aren't there quite a number of universities in China?"

"Yes, but there's a story to it. Jade's father is a doctor. He's the Chief of Medical Services at the Colorado School of Medicine. He's sponsoring Lee through undergraduate work and after that, through medical school. Lee's father is a doctor in Shanghai and he and Dr. Sando knew each other when Dr. Sando was head of the World Health Organization and was stationed there. Jade and her mother lived in Shanghai, too, but Jade was so young she doesn't remember very much about it."

"What a coincidence. It's a small world, isn't it? We'll look forward to meeting Lee. And where do Penny and Jade live?"

"They live in Denver, too, but Jade is away at the University of California, Berkeley, and won't be back home till May twenty-sixth. As a matter of fact, the two of you are a lot alike. You're a sophomore and she's a freshman, but you're both about the same age. Both short. And both of you have long, dark hair. Nobody would know the difference between you from half a block away."

"That's swell! We can trade clothes. We'll have a good time. When can you come to San Carlos?"

"We'll aim for June first, but I'll call you next week after I've talked with everyone."

The waiter brought our clam chowder and Crab Louis salads. We hardly noticed them and barely stopped talking long enough to eat. Bill, naturally, asked Eric technical questions about scuba diving, but I wanted to hear the stories of Eric's diving adventures in seas all around the world, even though I'd heard them before.

Suddenly I noticed the old clock by the ship's compass on the wall. "Oh, where'd the time go? I'm supposed to meet Professor Whitney in twenty minutes. I've got to run. Call me as soon as you can tell us anything more."

I picked up the check and placed two bills with it. "Courtesy of Dad. Next time, it'll be Maria doing the cooking. She makes a bouillabaisse to die for, it's so heavenly."

We walked out to the busy curb. I stretched up on my tiptoes and pecked Eric on the cheek, then kissed Bill on the lips. "Bye, you two. This was great. I can hardly wait to see you all in Mexico!"

Chapter 5.

The plane descended and the FASTEN YOUR SEAT BELT sign flashed on. My pulse beat faster in excitement. This was the first time I'd flown to Mexico by myself.

Out my window were the jagged, grotesque peaks that tumultuous volcanic and earthquake activity had formed ten million years ago. At their foot, the aqua Sea of Cortez shimmered in the sunshine, and dazzling white sailboats danced on the water. I felt an overwhelming sense of happiness and peace.

This sea symbolized the finest times of my life: vacations with my mother, father, and friends. My mind flashed back to sunny days when we dug for clams. Deep-sea fishing. Beach parties by a driftwood fire. Chasing phosphorescence like sparkling fireflies in the midnight surf. Happy childhood memories flooded my mind.

This time, without my parents, it would be different. I felt an ache of sorrow that so much had changed. "I'll miss you, Mom. You, too, Dad. It's never going to be the same again, is it? Mom, I wish you were here to meet Bill. You'd like him, he's so good. I'm going to spend the rest of my life with him, and I'm sure you would approve," I murmured.

"This is Captain Morales," came over the speaker. My attention snapped to the announcement. "My crew and I want to thank you for flying with us. We are descending from 30,000 feet and we will be landing at the Guaymas Aeropuerto in a few minutes. The temperature at the airport is 98 degrees, with an eight-mile-per-hour breeze blowing off the sea. High tide will occur at 7:18 tonight. We hope you will have a happy holiday in Mexico, and will fly again with us when you leave."

There was a rustle and a small commotion as passengers placed magazines in seat pockets, gathered packages and purses, and adjusted seatbacks to their upright position.

I realized I was anticipating our arrival in Guaymas with an eagerness I had not expected. Impatient to be on the ground, I unbuckled my seat-belt and hurried up the aisle the moment the plane stopped at the terminal.

Flight attendants slid the door open with a thud, and the rush of dry, suffocating desert heat took our breath away.

"Just be glad the humidity is low," I said to the heavy man who huffed across the tarmac beside me. "Once you get near the beach, there will be a cool, fresh breeze. You'll absolutely love it!"

It only took a moment to claim my baggage and carry it to the parking lot where Dad kept a car for family vacations. "I don't trust rented cars outside the U.S.," he always said. "You never know where it's been driven or when it's going to break down, and it's too hard to find help of any kind down here."

I stretched to lift my bags into the trunk, then leaned over and arranged them neatly. Just like I keep my desk, my room, and anything else I'm responsible for. "You're a compulsive neatener," Dad always complains. True. I've heard it's a form of insanity.

Eager to be on the highway, I begrudged the seconds it took to move the seat close enough that I could reach the brake and to adjust the steering wheel and mirror. I don't know why I wasn't born tall and svelte instead of five-one and a little too thin. They don't design anything for short shrimps. Especially skinny short shrimps.

I eased the car out of the parking lot and onto the main highway north, passed the poultry ranch, and took the cut-off to San Carlos, fifteen miles westward toward the sea. "Watch out, San Carlos. Here I come!" I shouted exultantly.

The two-lane black-top wound between summer-dry, brown, sandy hills dotted with desert vegetation: thorny ironwood, one-armed giant cardons that resembled Arizona saguaros, cholla cactus with needles that were fuzzy and light in the sunshine, and pale green palo de arco trees that have lovely, intricate yellow flowers. Tiny orange blossoms waved like miniature flags from the tips of the spiny, stick-like ocotillo.

Most people who come here think the Sonora Desert has a unique, magical beauty. So do I. There is nothing like this open space and freedom in Washington. Here, a person can really be alone and enjoy the magnificence of nature.

I could smell the fresh salt air and I felt newly alive. The first view of the sea would be around the next curve in the road. I accelerated, unable to wait, and there it was!

White surf foamed and roared ashore from the endless blue sea. My view of the mile-long beach was interrupted only by an occasional sand dune with tall grass blowing in the breeze.

Following the beach, I passed an estuary and a mangrove jungle where white, long-necked birds crooned haunting songs; new condominiums were nearby; and shallow clam beds where our family used to go at low tide to dig clams for supper. I thought, wouldn't it be fun to bring the whole gang here for clamming next week and have a clambake on the beach?

I slowed the car, opened the windows, and filled my lungs with the fresh, moist, warm-cool ocean air. It had been six months since my lungs had been so clean.

Somebody told me once that it takes fifty-six deep breaths to completely change the air in one's system. Accordingly, I opened my mouth wide, sucked in a large volume of air, and let it out in a great heave. "Out with pollution. In with pure air. Out with pollution. In with pure air..." I began to chant and count to fifty-six.

I was driving and sitting tall and straight, chest high, shoulders back, mouth opened wide, drawing huge breaths of air into my lungs, then pursing my lips and blowing the air out with deep heaves, collapsing my chest and shoulders.

An old, rusty, rattley pick-up truck passed me, and two men, Mexicans, stared at me, their mouths gaping open. After they passed, they turned around and stared some more, then drove on, speeding up and shaking their heads.

I didn't have to understand Spanish to comprehend what "*poco loco* Americano" meant when I read their lips, and I'm sure they hoped I wouldn't get anywhere near their wives or children. "Crazy American."

Oh, well.

I giggled, inhaled deeply, and resumed, "Forty-two, forty-three.....

Chapter 6.

Happy to be near the ocean again, I sped around the bend in the road toward the yacht club, pulled into the dirt parking lot and stepped out of the car. How peaceful it was! Only the sounds of boats rocking gently in the bay, seagulls mewing, and pieces of conversations in Spanish carried across the quiet water.

What a difference from Washington with its world-shaking decisions and traffic. And crime.

I stood on the weathered, splintered planks of the dock, letting my hair blow in the breeze.

The bay, surrounded by bluffs that sheltered it from storms, was filled with sailboats, a seaborne forest of masts. Moored farther out were luxurious yachts: there was SANS SOUCI. Tied to the docks, cushioned from bumping too hard against the weathered planks, were the inboard/outboards; run-abouts—that one said WYF'S MINK—; and dinghies. It was great to be back!

"Are you looking for your boat?" a man called from the marina office.

I looked up the hill.

"Roberto, how nice to see you! Yes, but I don't find it," I answered the owner of the marina.

"We have it moored out in the bay where it can't rub against the dock," Roberto said, walking down the slope. "Do you want me to bring it in for you?"

"Yes, would you, please? But I don't need it 'til tomorrow. I'd like to go on up to the house right now and get it opened up. We have guests coming, and I have some things to do before they get here."

"Very good," Roberto answered. "Will the senator be here?"

"No, not this time. But he said to tell you hello and thank you for looking after the boat."

"No problem. I'm always at his service. And yours," Roberto answered, tipped his sailor's cap respectfully, and walked with me to my car. "You have a good evening, Miss Shepard. I'll have your boat ready for you the first thing tomorrow."

He opened the car door for me and waved goodbye. I drove out of the parking area, up the steep hill, and around the end of the rocky, cactus-studded peninsula with its cliff that overhung the sea.

There, on the highest point of the cliff, was our white, rambling house. I caught my breath at the view: the cloudless, blue sky punctuated with soaring white seagulls, the shimmering aqua water far below, and the wild, jagged peaks of the Tetas de Cabra across the bay.

This was exactly what I needed, I knew. I could hardly wait to share it with Bill and the others, but I was also going to enjoy these first few days all by myself. There would be time to run on the beach and swim, maybe even do a little fishing.

I parked beside the wrought-iron lamp posts with the crackled amber globes along the circular driveway in front of the arched entryway. The entryway and windows were covered with Mexican grillwork designed for beauty, but also for security against entry, not that anyone would ever try to break in, I remembered Dad saying.

Lugging my bags up the walkway, I paid attention to the yard. It didn't look right. The ice plants, succulents which are especially hardy in the sea air, had overgrown the planters and had overrun the flagstone walk.

Vines trained to cling gracefully to trellises against the house now grew wildly over the roof and cascaded off the edge, fuchia blossoms swinging in the sea breeze. The Mexican fan palms also suffered from neglect, and the ground under the flame trees was covered with dead and broken limbs.

Our waterfall of volcanic rocks was turned off and the goldfish pond was filled with dead leaves.

Something was very much wrong! Where was Pablo? He'd always kept the yard and garden in perfect shape. We could arrive without notice and the house and grounds would be immaculate.

I fished in my purse for the door key and let myself into the house.

At least the inside looked fine. That was a relief! Maria had been here and kept the house clean, but I wondered again where Pablo was. Could he be sick? Wouldn't he have sent someone else if he were? It was not like him to neglect the place.

I knew now what I'd be doing during the next few days, and it wouldn't be swimming or fishing.

I walked through the long living room that overlooked the bay. One by one, I unlocked the windows and let the fresh sea breeze sweep through, then opened the doors and windows in the rest of the house.

Ummm, all that salt air smelled good!

There wasn't any food in the refrigerator, so I wrote a small grocery list for tonight and tomorrow morning. I'd quickly unpack my clothes and go to the little neighborhood market this evening. After Maria arrived here at noon on Tuesday we'd make up a bigger list that she could take to Guaymas. She had her own favorite produce stalls, bakeries and meat markets where she knew everybody and they knew her. Market day was a social occasion as much as anything else.

I had already decided that the first thing I was going to ask Maria when she got here was if she knew what had happened to Pablo.

Chapter 7.

The sun had risen the next morning before I awakened to the sound of surf softly slapping against the cliff. For a few moments I didn't know where I was. Where was the roar of traffic on the expressway? The clattering of trash cans, dumpsters and sanitation trucks?

Then I remembered and smiled to myself. Of course! Bahía San Carlos, Mexico.

I pulled on my favorite old, faded shorts and shirt, slipped into tattered deck shoes and threw open the bedroom door to the terrace.

Over the bay, gulls, cormorants and frigates plummeted from the sky at breakneck speed and splashed into a wild feeding frenzy of silvery mackerel that flashed and thrashed in the bright sunlight. Brown pelicans scooped up fish crosswise in their bills and flew a short distance, landed on the water and gulped them down.

Fascinated, I hurried across the flagstone terrace to the stone steps which led fifty feet down the cliff to the water's edge. The stairway was steep, even with three landings and switchbacks. Mother always said to everyone, "Be careful when you do down those steps. You could get killed if you fell down them."

I was careful as I hurried down.

At the bottom was a small private cove of clean white sand, ideal for sunning and swimming, and a hundred sand castles built and washed away over the years.

At each end of the cove were great red boulders which had broken from the cliff many years ago and crashed into the sea.

Our scarred and weathered dinghy rested upside down on the sand above tide line, waiting only for a fisherman to right it and push it into the bay. As much as I wanted to, it wasn't going to be me. At least not right away. I had work to do.

Compulsive, I allowed myself only five minutes by the sea, then climbed the steps to the terrace. I looked longingly at the view, turned, and stomped into the kitchen to make something to eat before I would start working on the yard.

I sliced a guava and a pineapple, spread of touch of butter on a freshly baked bolillo, and made a cup of strong Mexican coffee.

Why did I feel so pressured to work on the yard? So what if I didn't get it ready before company came? They weren't going to be critical. Why couldn't I just relax and enjoy myself?

I ate quickly, wrapped the left-over fruit and put it in the refrigerator, washed my plate and cup, and went outdoors to the carport storage room for a ladder and pruning tools.

Looking at the neglected yard, my thoughts returned to Pablo. How could he have let the vines become so overgrown? They hadn't been pruned for months. If he wasn't going to work for us any more, why didn't he let us know?

Perturbed, I carried the ladder and pruning shears to the back terrace, climbed into the top of a bougainvillea vine, and began cutting away the overgrowth. Wispy spider webs tangled themselves around my hands and face. Dry, dusty leaves caught in my hair, and heavy, scratchy vines fell onto my arms and shoulders.

The dust and pollen were so thick they made my eyes cloudy and gave me a fit of sneezing. Perspiration soaked my hair and drops of salty moisture dripped off the stray wisps which fell loose from my hairclasp. Why wasn't Pablo here to do this?

Suddenly I had one of those funny feelings people sometimes get when they sense that they're not alone. A sense of uneasiness or premonition.

Was it a footstep I heard? A small rock kicked? Pablo coming? Or Maria? Or was I just hearing things?

I threw an armful of butchered vines to the ground. Certain now that someone really was behind me, I snapped my head over my shoulder to look.

Directly behind me stood a man I'd never seen before; a squat, husky, dark-skinned man. His crumpled, soiled shirt, buttons loose or lost, was open at the neck. A gold and silver medal of St. Peter, the Great Fisherman, dangled from a heavy chain. The man's baggy cotton pants were tied with a hank of rape where a belt should have been. On his filthy, crusty feet he wore huaraches, native sandals woven of narrow strips of leather with traditional soles cut from old rubber tires.

My heart thumped and jolted. I was too startled and frightened to even breathe.

Who was this man? What did he want?

"Good Morning, Miss. I am Juan," the man said. A gruesome smile bared brown and broken teeth. Reddened, watery eyes looked out of an unshaved face.

"My name is Juan," he said again, watching me.

"Juan?" I questioned, trying to regain my voice.

"Yes, Juan."

"Juan who? What are you doing here?" I demanded, a little braver.

"Just Juan. I am your gardener," the man said.

Cautiously, I climbed down the ladder, holding the pruning shears ready to defend myself if the man made any move.

"Where's Pablo? He's our gardener."

"Gone."

"Gone where?" I asked.

"Just gone. He will not be back. Ever."

Suspicious and wary, I asked, "How do you know Pablo won't be back?"

"The Man, he told me Pablo will not be back."

"The Man? What man? I don't know what you're talking about. Pablo is our gardener and I think you better leave." I was trying to keep the trembling out of my voice and sound as though I was in control, but I didn't think I was going to be able to pull it off. I sure wished Dad were here!

The stocky man shifted his weight, pulled his dirty Panama lower on his forehead, casting his face in shadow, and spat on the flagstones. "I will not leave. The Man say for me to come here. Today. He say you will be alone and I am to watch you. He told me to take care of you. I will stay."

Almost in a panic, I lied, "I'm not alone. Maria will be right back, and my father just left for a moment."

"Okay. So I take care of everybody. Now give me your pruning shears and I will make your garden beautiful," the determined man said. He turned and walked to the carport storage room as though he knew exactly what was in it, opened the door, and took out a shovel and rake.

"You go clean the house. I will clean the yard Juan ordered. With a slight but noticeable limp, he slowly shuffled around the corner of the house, his leather huaraches squeaking as he walked.

Juan? Just Juan? Who was he? Who sent him? Was the man evil? How did anyone know I'd be here alone today? Was there a perfectly good explanation or was I in trouble?

Taking no chances, I hurried into the house and locked the doors and windows.

Why am I so jumpy, I wondered. *This is the safest place I've ever known. A few petty thefts— cameras, watches on the beach—but that's all. I must be hyper from living in the city all year. Maybe Dad's right: maybe I do need a vacation.*

When Maria gets here, perhaps she'll know who Juan is. Will she know who The Man is, too? She better hurry, because there's no way I'm going to unlock this house until somebody gets here even if I starve.

Chapter 8.

The moment I heard tires crunch on the gravel driveway I hurried to the living room window to see who was there. A van stopped and the driver looked at the house to make sure it was the right one.

I raced outside as Eric leaped from the van. I threw my arms around him like a long-lost brother. "Eric, I'm so glad you're here!" I exclaimed in relief.

Pleased at the reception, but puzzled, too, he looked at me acutely and said, "We're glad to be here. Are you all right?"

"Oh, sure. Fine," I answered breezily. "Just glad you made it okay."

A youngish woman and a guy and girl about my age stepped down from the van.

"Velvet, I want you to meet everybody. This is Sandy Allen," Eric said, motioning her forward. "Sandy, Velvet Shepard."

"Hi. I'm pleased to meet you," I said. She had beautiful, long, copper-colored hair that shot off fireworks as the sunshine reflected off it. She was almost as tall as Eric and had a lovely shape. I'd heard Eric tell Bill that Penny had the figure of an hourglass at eight A.M. Now I knew what he meant.

Sandy's complexion was pure ivory and almost transparent. "With skin like yours," I said, "we better keep you in sunscreen, long sleeves and big hats."

"You must be Jade Sando," I said to the girl standing beside Sandy. "You really are my twin. From fifty feet away, no one will be able to tell us apart."

Enormous, dark, doe-like eyes smiled. "Yes, that's me, and I'm happy to meet you. I've heard a lot about you. Thank you for inviting us to share your vacation."

Jade was not much over five feet tall and I doubted if she weighed a hundred pounds. Her hair was thick and dark, worn swept back into a French braid, doubled up and fastened with a silver and turquoise barrette.

I noticed her prominent cheekbones and wondered if she, like me, had some Indian ancestry. A few generations back in my family, a tall, thin English settler married a small-boned Cherokee woman. She was my great-grandmother. They both passed their slender builds from one generation to the next, and my great-grandmother passed along her cheekbones.

Jade's features were somewhat stronger than mine. Was she of Pueblo or Navajo heritage? I'd ask her when I got a chance.

Eric picked up the introductions again. "This is Lee Long of Shanghai and Denver." "Lee, welcome to Mexico. We'll try to give you a vacation that's different from any others you've known. One you'll always remember," I said.

Lee was taller than other Chinese boys I knew at school, but he had the same slender build and clear, smooth skin.

His straight, black hair was slightly shaggy around his collar, and unruly wisps of spikey bangs fell across his broad forehead. When he looked at me and said hello, it was as though he could see into my very soul. I liked him instantly.

"Is Bill here yet?" Eric asked and reached into the van to hand the luggage out to Lee.

"No, but his plane comes in at three o'clock this afternoon. How would you all like to unpack and drink some of Maria's fresh limeade, and then go to the airport with me? I can show you around the area on the way," I answered. "Eric, you've been to San Carlos before, but you might not know some of my favorite places, and all of them will be knew to everyone else."

Simultaneously, Eric and Sandy said, "We'd really like that."

"Two thoughts but as one," Sandy laughed. "Just show us where to drop our stuff."

I led them out of the heat into the cool house.

"That's an exquisite view of the sea!" Sandy exclaimed. "Is it all right if I do some painting from your terrace someday soon?"

"Sure," I answered, "but there are so many-beautiful scenes around here, it'll be difficult to choose which ones to paint. How would you like to do one for us to hang over the fireplace?"

"I'd be pleased to, but maybe you should see my work before you make the invitation. You might decide to put it inside the fireplace instead of over it," Sandy said, laughing.

"No, you won't," Jade cut in. "Sandy's paintings are so good there's a waiting list of galleries wanting her work. I keep telling her she should stop teaching art in high school and paint fulltime."

Sandy smiled. "Jade was one of my students and she's a pretty good artist herself."

I took my guests through the living room with its highly polished brick floor, thanks to Maria, and the soft leather chairs and sofas. There were hand-carved coffee tables, and amber lamps that were crafted for my mother when she first furnished the house.

We entered a corridor of bedrooms facing the sea.

"Sandy, would you like to have this first room? Jade, I thought you and I could share the next one, if that's all right with you. Eric, could you and Lee take the room next to us, and we'll give Bill the one on the end," I suggested as we came to each door.

"That's great," Eric said, and everyone nodded in agreement. "Where do you want us to store the diving equipment and wet suits?"

"Come with me to the carport. There's a big storage room that you can drive right up to."

They placed their bags in their rooms, then helped Eric move the diving gear into the storage room and arrange it neatly along the wall.

"Now, come meet Maria," I said. "She has a pitcher of fresh limeade ready for us."

They followed me into the large, sun-drenched kitchen filled with the tempting fragrance of Maria's bouillabaisse bubbling in a clay pot.

"Have a seat," I said and motioned for them to sit at the round, carved dining table in the bay window. It had a spectacular 180-degree view of the sea, sky, and mountain peaks. My family lived around this table practically all the time, looking at the view, talking, reading, or watching Maria cook.

I put my arm through Maria's and pulled her to the table. "I want you to meet our marvelous Maria, the world's best cook and housekeeper. If there's anything you want, she can cook it, make it, do it or get it."

She smiled self-consciously. She knew I was sincere, but praise always flustered her. She fingered the tiny gold cross on the chain around her neck, the cross my mother had removed from her own neck and fastened around Maria's the last time Mother was here. "Look after yourself," she had said, "and look after my baby, too."

Maria, diminutive with thinning hair streaked with gray, has smile lines etched in her tranquil face. She always wears a black fringed shawl over her narrow shoulders, even in the summertime. "The sea air makes my bones ache," she explains.

Maria has been with us forever. She watched me as a tiny tyke catching starfish and building castles in the sand. One day she said to my mother, "I would give my life for that child. She is like my own. I could love her no more if she were."

Maria poured fresh icy limeade into cobalt blue glasses Mother and I had bought from a glass-blower in Tlaquepaque last summer. She placed them on the brilliantly-striped serape on the table.

Everybody asked questions non-stop about San Carlos and Guaymas, deep-sea fishing and diving, the sea life, and the geography of the area.

"Whoa, you guys! That's enough questions. You've already earned one credit in San Carlos 101 and you've only been here an hour," I said. "Why don't we finish our limeade and start the lab course? Let's go see some of the country and pick up Bill at the airport."

"Sure," Sandy said. "Maria that was wonderful. You'll have to give me your recipe."

"I'll open an import business and keep you supplied with limes," Eric said to Sandy.

"And we'll be over every day after school," the rest of us added as we got up from the table.

Chapter 9.

All of us talking at once, we climbed into Eric's van to go sightseeing on the way to Guaymas Airport. I appointed myself as tour guide, but I did make one concession. "Eric," I said, "you've been here before, so if I miss something, or if I slip into overkill, be sure and interrupt me. I tend to get carried away."

We wound through the residential area on the peninsula, and down the hill past the cantina and the yacht club. "On your right," I pointed, "is the Posado de San Carlos where my family used to stay before we built our house. The hotel rooms open onto the beach, and there's an elegant dining terrace that overlooks the sea. The moon will be full in a few days, and I'd like to bring you here for dinner. Afterwards, we can walk barefooted on the beach, our souls in tune, and watch the moonlight turn the sea from black to gold lame."

"Velvet, that's a lovely, romantic phrase. I didn't realize you were poetic," Sandy said, somewhat skeptically.

"That was lovely, wasn't it? I borrowed it from a book of seaside poetry."

"No-o-o! I don't believe this girl," Eric groaned. "And to think Bill is committed to marry her! I think he *should* be committed."

Unabashed, I resumed my self-appointed role as tour guide. I pointed ahead and said, "Across the road to your left is the country club. Don't you like the shady terraces and white arches? The delicate bougainvillea blossoms contrasting with giant elephant-ear philodendrons? The red tile roof and wrought-iron grillwork? It's quite representative of Mexico, don't you think?

"Now, Eric, turn off on the first road to the right and I'll show everyone our other resort area," I directed. We circled through a community of white slump brick houses with more of the clay tile roofs.

Sandy observed the colorful panorama of white homes with green trees and vines against a background of blue ocean and sky, looking with the eyes of an artist alert for scenes to paint. She turned to Jade, and speaking as Jade's art teacher, said, "Jade, do you remember the discussion we had a few days ago about the necessity for an artist to refine his powers of observation, his ability to notice and remember details? Well, here's a good example of variations in a common thing, trees."

We scrutinized the trees Sandy pointed to.

"Discern the variations in the leaves alone: their size, shape, thickness, coloration. Look for contrasts in texture, too, because you'll use your brushes differently to depict them."

"Yes, I see what you mean. What kind of trees are they?" Jade asked.

Eric answered, "The trees with the fiddle-shaped, heavy, dark green leaves are fig trees. The ones with the small, pointed, pale green leaves are limes or lemons. That particular type of palm tree is a date palm; see the cluster of tiny dates forming in the fronds? And you probably recognize the banana trees."

"If you want to, Jade, we can paint together while we're here. In the meantime, I'd like for you to pay close attention to everything and everybody you see. Watch for those discriminating details that are unique to each object or person," Sandy said. "Remember them clearly enough that you can reproduce them on canvas later."

"What are those tall plants growing against the houses...the ones with the pointed leaves?" Jade asked.

"Poinsettias," I answered. "They grow to half the height of the houses, and at Christmas time they turn brilliant red. Most of these homes were built by Americans who use them during the winter months— they're all deserted now—and the poinsettias are about the only thing around here that look anything like an American Christmas."

Jade pointed to the cluster of homes and yards. "These homes are built so close to the water the yards drop straight down to the sea. What happens when there are storms? Or don't you get storms in San Carlos?"

"We do, but this bay is fairly well protected and the surf hardly ever gets high enough to cause flooding. It's the unprotected bays and out on the open sea where the water becomes wild," Eric explained.

Sandy, appreciating the natural beauty of the area, said, "I love the sand-swept desert and the rough, raw grandeur of those mountains. Some of them look like uplifted granite faults. I hope no real estate developer turns this spectacular seacoast into another Acapulco with wall-to-wall high-rise hotels and condos along the beach."

We drove back up to the main road toward a small settlement on the shore. "What kind of village is that?" Sandy asked.

"That's a Yaqui Indian village," Eric answered and slowed the van so we could look at it. The huts were built of mangrove roots, organ pipe cactuses, corrugated, rusty tin sheeting, and gunny sacks.

Children ran to the road, waved and smiled. Red Rhode Island hens pecked in the dirt, searching for grain that had been scattered, and fat pigs slept in the meager shade. On the shore, fishermen with their pants' cuffs rolled up pulled long, wooden boats filled with piles of fish netting and red cans of gasoline out of the bay and onto the clean sand.

"I just have to paint that scene!" Sandy-exclaimed. "Will they mind?"

"When you're ready, we'll ask them," Eric said.

As tour guide, I pointed out beautiful, peaceful Bahia San Francisco at the base of the rugged mountains, the dark, mysterious mangrove jungle and the estuary, and all the places I wanted to bring everyone to dig clams, catch crabs, hunt seashells and come diving.

"Velvet," Jade stopped me, "you're so enthusiastic, it's infectious. How can we possibly get to do everything in just three weeks?"

"Oh, you really can't. You'll want to keep coming back for the rest of your life," I said. "Even after all the years I've been coming here, I still have new experiences every time. Just wait. You will, too. You'll see."

Chapter 10.

Eric drove into the airport parking lot only moments before the sleek, silvery airliner bringing Bill touched down on the sizzling tarmac.

"Quick! Let's be at the gate when Bill comes off the plane," I said and hurried into the terminal reception area. People waiting to greet friends and relatives clustered in small, excited groups.

We pressed against the plate-glass windows and watched the airliner roll to a stop. The ground crew positioned a rolling stairway to connect to the plane, and the forward door slid open.

A full load of passengers deplaned and, one by one, grasped the metal railing of the stairs and descended the narrow steps to the ground. We glanced at each passenger, watching for Bill. Children in shorts and T-shirts, teenagers in jeans and sandals, parents impatiently shepherding them, obvious newlyweds and businessmen in tropical suits hurried across the tarmac and entered the terminal.

None of them were my fiancé.

"Where's Bill?" I asked, becoming anxious. "He should have gotten off the plane by now."

"Take a look at the guy at the top of the stairs," Eric said. We studied the man.

"Where? I don't see him."

"There. In the tan cotton shirt, baggy khaki pants and suede desert boots. That's him," Eric pointed.

"No, that's not Bill. He always wears suits and white shirts, or at least coordinated slacks and polos," I said with absolute certainty.

"Look again," Eric teased.

The man was about Bill's size, I had to admit. I couldn't see his hair under the wide-brimmed hat he wore, but the clean-shaved face was Bill's, all right.

Flabbergasted, I said, "I can't believe it! Is that laid-back slouch the same dynamic go-getter who draws up multi-million-dollar sales contracts for my dad?"

"The same," Eric laughed. "You might be surprised by a lot of things about that guy when you get to know him better. This trip will probably be good for you. Maybe for him, too."

I wondered, what did he mean by that? It seemed to me that we knew each other fairly well. We were engaged, after all.

Bill walked briskly across the tarmac and into the reception area. Still somewhat dumbfounded, I nevertheless rushed into his arms. "Bill, I've missed you. I'm so glad you're here!"

Aware of the people smiling at my exuberance, Bill unwrapped my arms from around his neck and took my hand. Inch by inch, we sidled through the crowd toward our group.

"I want you to meet everyone. This is Sandy Allen."

"So pleased to finally meet you," Bill said.

I indicated Lee and said, "This is Lee Long of Shanghai."

"Hi. I'm happy to know you," Lee said and shook Bill's hand.

"And this is my twin, Jade Sando."

"She really is your twin. We'll have to be careful or we'll all be in trouble," Bill said.

"I'm glad to meet you," Jade said warmly. "I feel as though I already know you, after all the things Velvet has told us about you."

"How was your flight? Do you have any bags?" Eric asked as we proceeded toward the baggage claim area.

Bill claimed his one bag and we hurried to the van.

"Now that everybody's here, what's the grand plan?" Eric asked. "When do you want to learn to dive?"

"I have some ideas," I offered. "Let's go get the van and I'll tell you on the way home."

Chapter 11.

Eric wheeled the van out of the airport parking lot. "I think we should spend this evening just letting you get unpacked, maybe take a swim at sunset, and eat one of Maria's wonderful dinners," I said. "You can go to bed early and let the sound of the surf lull you into a good sleep. Then, tomorrow I'll show you more of the countryside, and Eric can start teaching his diving course. Does that sound good?"

"You bet it does," Eric stated.

"It sounds fine to me, too," Sandy said.

"Then let's go straight home. This vacation is going to be outstanding! The experience of a lifetime," I proclaimed.

"Velvet, your yard is beautiful," Sandy said as we drove into the driveway. "How do you keep all your greenery so perfectly manicured? Do you have help or do you do it yourself?"

I sighed. "Yes. No. I don't know. We did have a super gardener, Pablo. For years. He kept the yard absolutely perfect whether we were here or not. Dad just sent him a check every month and didn't even have to tell him what to do. But when I got here the other day the yard looked terrible. Dead branches, broken palm fronds, vines growing wild. And, I got the scare of my life."

"What happened?" Bill asked at full attention.

"The yard looked so bad I decided I'd have to do the work myself, and while I was on top of the ladder pruning one of those bougainvillea vines on the back terrace, I thought I heard a noise. I turned around and some strange, ugly, mean-looking man was staring up at me. I thought I'd die, I was so scared."

"Who was he? What did he look like? What did he want?" Bill asked. Interrogated, actually.

Wasn't that just like a lawyer? Was that what I was going live with for the rest of my life?

"He said his name was Juan. Just Juan. And he said some man had told him to come here, that I would be alone, and he was to watch me and take care of me. I didn't know what he meant by 'taking care of me'. He wouldn't tell me who The Man was and he wouldn't go away. I lied and told him that Maria and Dad would be right back. I was sure wishing my father would walk in right then."

Everybody looked at me with uneasiness, and Bill looked alarmed. More than alarmed. More like furious. He clenched his teeth, those little muscles across his jaws were popping, and frown lines marked his brow. It seemed to me that he was over-reacting to an incident which was not all that serious. "Tell me what happened," Bill ordered.

"He told me to go clean the house and said he'd clean the yard. I ran in and locked the doors and stayed there 'til Maria arrived."

"What did she say when you told her about the man?" Bill asked.

"Maria said the people who live around here know Juan and say he hears voices no one else hears, and predicts events before they happen. They think he's rather strange and maybe a little bit psychic, but totally harmless," I quoted Maria.

"It still doesn't make any sense," Bill argued. "Why was he in your yard? Why did he say he was going to 'take care of you'? Where's your regular gardener, Juan?"

Bill's fists kept clenching and unclenching. Why was he so hyper? My dad wouldn't be. My dad always keeps his cool.

"Maria said she'd heard that Juan got sick and his daughter and her husband took him to Topolobampo to live with them. He'd be able to get the medical attention he needed in nearby Los Mochis," I explained. "So, I guess our new gardener is Pablo. At least 'til he hears another voice and goes there to scare somebody else out of their wits."

"Velvet, I should never have let you fly down here alone," Bill said angrily. Who was he angry at? Himself? Or me?

"But it's perfectly safe," I protested. "Nothing ever happens here. I'm just spooky from living in the city."

"Maybe so, but from now on, I don't want you to go anyplace alone," he stated.

"And that's final?" I asked, getting mad.

"And that's final!" he ordered. Where did he get off acting like that!

I cringed at his outburst and at what everyone must be thinking. It was upsetting enough to fight with the man I was going to marry, but it was especially bad in front of guests.

And anyway, the incident with Juan was not that big a deal. Why did Bill react like that? He was unreasonable. Was this aspect of his personality there all the time and I didn't know it? What else did I need to learn about this man?

Or was it possible there was more danger than I realized? Had crime taken over this place, too? Was I being naive and confused? And maybe unfair?

Chapter 12.

"Good morning," Lee Long shouted to Jade and me, and waved from the cove at the base of our cliff.

"Hi, Lee. You're out early, aren't you?" I shouted back.

"Yes, and look at that sunrise. Have you ever seen such brilliant reds and pinks in the morning sky?" He was speaking to both of us, but his eyes were on Jade, her fresh face, her hair brushed neatly into the French braid that was her signature.

Long-legged for a Chinese boy, Lee bounded up the steep flight of steps to the top of the cliff. With the easy grace and energy of a runner, he sprinted across the flagstone terrace to where Jade stood under dewy bougainvillea blossoms. He seemed awed as he absorbed the fragrance of the flowers and Jade's beauty.

Oh, hoh! A romance was blooming before my very eyes. This was going to be a fun summer.

"Would you like to run on the beach?" Lee asked. "We haven't run together since we were in China last summer. Our last run was on the Great Wall."

"Sure, we'd love to," Jade and I both answered.

Jade said, "The only running I've done this year was on the track at Berkeley. And one time on the beach out there. As our Denver friend Jeff would say, lezgo."

Wearing Lycra running shorts and tops and scuffed Adidas, we loped through the residential area, down the hill and onto the white sand of San Francisco Bay. Well matched, we set a brisk but comfortable pace. It was obvious that Jade and Lee were happy to run together again.

"This is as far as we can go," I said at the end of the mile-long arc of beach. "We'll either have to turn back or swim around that point."

"Let's climb on top where we can watch the last of the sunrise, and then take a quick swim before we run again," Jade suggested.

Lee climbed up the pile of jumbled, massive boulders, and reached down for Jade's hand and then mine.

Stepping carefully, we climbed to the top of the red rocks which overhung the bay, and watched the sea birds circling overhead, diving for their breakfast in the churning frenzy of splashing, silvery fish which were fleeing from larger fish below them.

Farther from the shore a school of dolphins, sleek and black, arched playfully in and out of the quiet sea. Lee watched, enchanted. "I've never seen open water before, or fish or dolphins, except in an aquarium."

Jade turned to look at Lee. "Do you miss Shanghai?"

"Oh, yes. The crowds on the streets, the noise and congestion, the wonderful smell of Chinese food cooking over coals. My family, most of all."

"How do you like living in Denver with my family?" she asked cautiously.

"I like it quite well, and I am very grateful to them. Your aunt looks after me just like my own mother would, and your father has already taken me to meet everybody in the medical school. By the time I can apply for entrance and take my exams and interviews,

I'll feel quite comfortable," Lee said. "Because of everything Dr. Sando is doing for me, my fortune cookie says YOU WILL BE A DOCTOR LIKE YOUR FATHER AND HIS FATHER BEFORE HIM."

Was that a twinge of envy Jade was feeling? Envy that her father and aunt in Denver could be with Lee every day, while she was way out on the California coast?

I was beginning to get a pretty clear picture of Jade and Lee. Lee was living in Jade's house, eating at her table, and talking with her family every night, but she wasn't getting to see him or talk to him because she was away at school. East meets West in a traditional conflict of love. How intriguing!

My first impression of Lee was that he was quiet and serious, and sensitive but reserved. His Chinese upbringing, probably.

He was obviously infatuated with Jade, and that had to create some problems. How would Jade's father and aunt look at it if the Chinese boy they were sponsoring for medical school became too affectionate with Jade? They might ship him off to Shanghai, and that would ruin everything.

Poor Lee!

Poor Jade!

Romeo and Juliet in the Space Age.

"How did you like your first year at Berkeley?" Lee asked politely. I had a hunch that wasn't what he really wanted to talk about, though. He was drinking her up with his eyes.

Jade answered Lee's question with enthusiasm. "Berkeley is great. My grades are good and I did well enough on the track team that they're giving me another scholarship for next year. I won a couple of new trophies and several ribbons, and our team holds the regional championship title."

"Are you still aiming for a degree in International Relations and then a law degree at Stanford?" Lee asked.

"More than ever, now that I've had a taste," Jade replied. "It's hard, but it's fascinating."

"And when you are an important briefcase-carrying lawyer and travel all over the world for your clients, will we meet in Beijing for another dinner at the 'Sick Duck' Restaurant like we promised when we were there?"

"Of course. I love Beijing," Jade said.

Go on, Jade, I wanted to say. Tell him you love him, too. But I didn't. I do have some couth, after all.

"You love Beijing except for the Summer Palace?" Lee asked.

In a single breath, their entire mood changed. Jade's smile died. Her eyes became damp. She shivered as if chilled. Silence hung heavy in the damp air.

What was that all about? What had happened that was so traumatic? Why did it affect them that way? When?

Chapter 13.

"Do you want to talk about it?" Lee asked softly. His attention focused totally on Jade. Neither of them seemed aware that I was there.

Jade stared blindly at the sea. Trembling. Remembering. What?

Lee laid his hand over hers and waited quietly.

I didn't move a muscle as the drama unfolded.

"I've never talked about it to anyone," Jade began. She took a deep breath, calmed her trembling "Not even my father. When he came to Beijing to watch us run on the Great Wall last summer, Eric told him what had happened so I wouldn't have to. Later, Dad talked with me about how to put bad events out of my mind and go on with my life. Events like when I was little and my mother died in Kuala Lampur, and like this thing with Scott. But I guess I haven't been very successful at doing it," she said sadly. "I've become suspicious and wary, even of people I know. That's not the way I want to live my life, never trusting anyone. Do you know what I mean?"

"Yes, I do know," Lee said. "Scott was a friend, a runner in your group. He went to your high school and was a big man on campus. A jock. Good-looking, intelligent, popular. How could you have guessed what he would turn into?"

Jade shuddered. "I relive those moments of lingering in the museum at the Summer Palace, admiring the fabulous treasures from an earlier reign, and daydreaming about what it must have been like to live in those days of opulence and grandeur."

She paused. "I can't ever forget standing and studying the artifacts. Suddenly, with no sound to warn me, someone slipped up behind me and threw incredibly strong arms around me. He crushed my ribs, and reached around to grab and twist my breasts with hands like a vice. Never in my life have I known that kind of pain. Or terror!" she cried.

"In my memory I hear again the words he snarled in that loud, deep voice of his. 'Now I've got you to myself, Jade. There's no one else around.'

"I was unable to believe what I was hearing, and unwilling to accept that it was true when I recognized that the voice belonged to Scott. Scott from my own school! A member of our team traveling and running in China. Susie's steady date."

Lee put his arm around Jade's shoulders.

"I was so terrified and frantic! I twisted and jerked as hard as I could 'til I broke loose. It took all I had, but I knew I had to run for my life."

I listened, sympathetic, spellbound, appalled.

"Scott caught me but he couldn't stop me. I was desperate, and somehow I had a surge of energy and plunged toward the exit. Scott was crazed and screaming threats, trying to drag me down. But he wasn't able to. Even with him gripping my arm and pulling me back, I managed to reach the heavy crimson door. I burst through it into the sunshine and straight into the middle of my team."

Jade shivered.

"Now, almost a year later, the memory still haunts me. It slips up on me during class, or when I'm running alone on the track. Even when surrounded by friends at a party. And how many times as I lie in bed at night?" she said pitifully.

Lee stroked her hand. "It's still terrible for you, isn't it?"

"Yes. I was so scared. And embarrassed," Jade said.

"Embarrassed? Why embarrassed? It wasn't your fault."

"No, but that's the way I felt. I felt as though I must have said something or done something that caused Scott to act the way he did. And I was miserable that I might ruin the whole China trip for everybody."

"And you didn't you talk to anyone about it? Not Sandy? Or Eric? Or a counselor at college?" Lee asked.

"No, I couldn't. You know how people are always joking about rape? Saying the victim asked for it? That it was her fault, and not the violator's? Well, I couldn't bear it if someone thought I had brought it on myself. So, I didn't ever talk to anyone about it. You're the only one. Can you understand how I feel?" Jade pleaded.

"Yes. I can understand. But there's something you need to know. Last September, after you left for college, your father did some investigating into Scott Carter's background. At first, all he learned was what a great guy on campus Scott was. But your father kept digging deeper and began to find out some things no one wanted to talk about."

"Like what?" Jade asked.

"Like Scott growing up in a home with a wealthy, alcoholic father who constantly humiliated him and beat him while his mother just stood and watched in silence. Never even tried to stop it. Just let it happen. Like neighborhood cats and dogs that disappeared from their yards, and later they were found on their front doorsteps, dead from poison or from slashed throats. And girlfriends who tried to stop Scott's advances on dates and were thrown out of the car, or smashed in the face. Or worse."

Jade's mouth fell open in shock. She stared at Lee, incredulous.

"That was Scott? Our Scott?"

"That was our Scott. Your father talked with a staff psychiatrist at the medical school and presented all the information he had collected. The psychiatrist said he couldn't make a diagnosis without spending time with Scott, but he did say he suspected that Scott is a psychopath and will continue to be dangerously violent. And do you want to know the funniest part of it? Well, not funny, really. But from what your father could find out, every girl Scott ever attacked was petite and had dark hair. Like his mother. Like you."

Lee became aware, finally, that I was still there and looked at me meaningfully. "And like you."

Jade shook her head sadly. "That is sick. What a tragedy. For everyone. What do you think ever happened to him?"

Lee said, "Scott told Eric, after you collapsed, that he was going to get out of China and go to Hawaii for a while. He said he didn't want to go home to Denver, and didn't want to go back to college in Boulder. Did anyone in your group hear from him after that?"

"Not that I know of. And I hope we never do!" Jade said vehemently.

"I hope we never do, either. Now, how about a swim? The water off this rocky point is deep and clear. We can dry out on the run back home, and by the time we get there Maria might have a hot breakfast waiting. Ready?" Lee asked and reached out his hands.

I felt an overwhelming tenderness and warmth for these two kids who shared a bad experience but could have so many good times ahead of them. I hoped they'd never have any more scary times. At least they'd be safe here, thanks be.

Chapter 14.

"Here's what I propose," Eric said as we finished breakfast. The basket of tortillas hot off Maria's grill was empty and nothing was left of the Omelet Mexicano or the sliced pineapple and papayas in the terra cotta bowl.

"Let's unpack the diving equipment and spread it out in the shade of the carport. Sandy and I can fit the diving masks, tunics, boots and fins to you, and demonstrate how to put on the buoyancy compensator. We can show you how to adjust them for a proper fit. Velvet, we used Jade as a model for you since you're about the same size. Your outfit is fluorescent blue and Jade's is passionate pink, but if you don't like those colors you can trade with each other."

I said to Jade, "Let's trade sometimes just for the fun of it, okay?"

"Sure. Love to," she agreed.

"Bill, we took your measurements to Watersports, Inc., the dive shop in Albuquerque. Peaches Hines and Richard Borden helped us select your gear. We think it will fit well, but you'll have to try it and see. "

"Sounds good," Bill said.

"I want to show you the other parts of the air system and demonstrate how to use them," Eric continued.

"What do you mean by an air system?" I asked.

"That's your buoyancy compensator, regulator, mouthpiece, hoses and air tanks."

Eager to become the next Jacques Cousteau, I asked, "When will we actually begin diving?"

"Soon. My plan is this: during the hot hours of each day we'll do the academic training. The classwork. At night you'll have time to study the dive manuals. We brought one for each of you. Then, every morning while it's still cool and the sea is calm, we'll work in the water."

"How long will that take?" I pressed. I wasn't being pushy, but it was hard to wait.

Eric glanced at me with that please-be-patient look my father was always giving me. Bill nodded his head in support of Eric.

I laughed. "Okay. I get the message. I'll do my homework. But when do we get to play?"

Sandy shook her head in exasperation, a look of kids-and-their-priorities on her face.

Eric grinned. "Are you by any chance related to a Senator Shepard? The originator of the Do-It-Now School of Thought?"

"I give up. Issue our orders," I conceded.

"What do you say about going fishing at dusk, cookouts on the beach at sundown, or dinners in the moonlight at the cantina or hotels? But no late nights, and no margaritas or tequila sunrises after tonight. If you'll pardon the parody, if you're going to drink, don't dive."

Jade said, "That's no problem. We're not really into drinking anyway. We're runners. And if we work as hard at learning to dive as it sounds like we will, we won't want to stay up late."

Lee and Sandy nodded agreement. Bill asked me with his eyes if that would be all right with me.

"Great," I said. "When do we start?"

There was a collective sigh of relief. I guess I was being a pain. I'd stop that right now. I certainly didn't want to come across as a spoiled brat.

"Then let's help Maria clear the table and go get the gear," Eric said and slid his chair back.

I looked at Eric, surprised and pleased. "How considerate of you. I'll bet your mother thought you were a sweet and precious little boy."

"Yes, she did, and I grew up to be a lovely adult," Eric said with a straight face.

"Oh, GET us OUT of here!" Bill groaned and scrambled to his feet. The rest of us were quick to follow.

Maria, surprised and pleased at Eric's offer to help, wore an enormous smile. It was clear that Eric was going to get all the sample tastings of every delicacy from her kitchen, and fresh limeade to his heart's content.

"Some men sure do have a way with women," I grumped and carried my dishes to the sink.

Chapter 15.

Enthusiastically, we carried the diving gear from the storage room to the shaded carport floor and arranged it for Eric to demonstrate.

"Let's do the fittings first," Eric suggested.

Sandy helped Jade and me into our colorful wet-suits and boots, adjusted the swim fins to fit over the boots, and showed us how to attach our weight belts and a complicated vest-like device.

"What's this for?" I asked.

Sandy said, "It's a buoyancy compensator: a flotation device. Eric will explain all about it during the academic portion of your training course. Now, as soon as I fasten these straps and buckles so the device is snug, he'll check it. Everything must fit exactly right before you go into the water because if it's too loose ..."

Sandy's words were lost in the roar of a car careening around the curve past the driveway and stirring up a storm of dust that enveloped us and settled thickly over our diving equipment.

"Oh! That makes me so mad!" I snapped. "Nobody has any business racing through this neighborhood. Whoever that was obviously has no respect for anyone else."

"That's true, but I'll bet there's one in every neighborhood," Sandy said. "Eric, would you check these adjustments for Velvet and Jade? See if they're snug enough."

Eric inspected the straps and buckles on my equipment. "That's a good fit," he pronounced. Let's look at Jade's."

I stepped out of the way toward the front of the carport, and knelt down to examine the air tanks; but, my attention was diverted by the sound of a car laboring up the hill. Our house was the last one on the road and it was unusual to have very much traffic. I was already irritated at the driver who'd passed a few minutes earlier, and this time I was ready to run out to the road and yell at him if he sped past our house.

The car didn't speed, though. It slowly eased around the curve and ground almost to a stop in front of our driveway. The driver appeared to be searching for someone or for a particular house number, but the moment he saw me scowling at him, he swung his face away, gunned the motor and sped over the hill.

"That's the same car that zoomed past here a while ago! I don't know what kind of car it was, and I couldn't tell who was driving—there's not any way to keep track of who lives in a resort community with people coming and going all the time—but I'm going to be watching for this guy!" I fumed.

"What did he look like?" Bill asked.

"Oh, I couldn't tell, but I'm going to keep my eyes peeled for him, and if he shows up here or anyplace else, I'm going to confront him!"

"I think I'd know him if I saw him again," Jade interrupted. "He had longish sun-bleached hair, no shirt, wide shoulders and a deep suntan. He's maybe a surfer or a football player...he has sort of an athletic look, you know? And the car was a '79 or '80 Ford sedan with a rusty dent in the front left fender. It was the same car that passed earlier."

"Jade, you're paying more attention to details than I thought," Sandy said, pleased with her student.

"He probably saw that he discovered a nest of beauties and couldn't resist coming back for a second look. Don't let it get to you. We're your admirers, too, and we'll keep you so surrounded with our strong, strapping, attentive brawn no one else will be able to get close," Eric said, trying to placate me. "Now let's go to work. It's class time."

Eric began showing the delicate diving instruments and explaining how they worked. I listened with only half my attention.

The other half was thinking: I'd noticed Pablo raking leaves near the carport while we were having our equipment fitted, as if he were eavesdropping.

At the time, I wondered why he seemed so interested in overhearing our conversation. Then, each time the car roared past, Pablo got a terrible, black frown on his face.

Did that car mean something to him? Who was the driver? Who was he looking for? Was Pablo in cahoots with him? What did that have to do with us?

I shook my head. I was becoming paranoid about Pablo. A couple of meaningless incidents and I was a nut-case.

It must be time for a swim, I thought. *Some physical activity.* I always felt better when I was active. But instead, it was time for class and I'd already missed part of Eric's lecture. "If you want to be a scuba diver, you can't just jump in," he was saying. "You have to know everything about your equipment and how to use it safely, and you have to understand the complexities of the sea."

I put the tan Ford out of my mind.

Chapter 16.

"This may seem complicated at first, but it'll begin to make sense when you study your dive manuals," Eric said as he demonstrated the scuba equipment. "By the time we finish the academic portion of this course, you'll feel comfortable with the technical aspect of scuba diving and be ready to enter the water."

"My head was already swimming with all this information. I was having brain strain. "Can we take a break?" I asked.

"Sure. In fact, why don't we stop for a few hours and go to the marina? We need to have a good look at your boat, run it on open sea, and get a feel for how it handles before we begin to dive from it."

"Terrific!" I exclaimed. "We can pack a picnic lunch and go up the coast to Algodones Beach."

"Great idea," Eric said.

We filled baskets with cheese and summer sausage, and bolillos and fruit, and loaded the ice chest with cold drinks.

"Jade, will you get the beach blankets out of the hall closet while we take the food to the van?" I asked.

In the carport, Eric said, "Let's move the diving equipment into the storage room and lock it up 'til we get back."

Pablo the Gardener, watching from the fishpond at the far end of the yard, called, "I will help you." He laid down his tools, limped across the yard to the carport and picked up an air tank.

Surprised, I watched him carry the tank into the storage room and return. Feet wide apart, Pablo planted himself solidly in front of me and asked, "How long will you be gone?"

"Two or three hours, I imagine. Why?"

"I will stay here 'til you get back. I will be your guard. Nothing bad will happen today," he said.

Why would anything bad happen today or any other day? Why was Pablo so mysterious and dramatic? Why did he think he had any powers to see into the future? He acted like he knew something I didn't know. Something ominous. He gave me the creeps.

In the van, Eric asked, "Where did you say Pablo came from? He seems awfully concerned about watching the house and the equipment."

"Yes, and watching me. I can't go anyplace that he doesn't show up. Maria doesn't know where Pablo comes from or where he goes when he leaves here, or anything else about his present life. But she did say that when Pablo was a young man he was captain of his own commercial shrimp boat. One day a typhoon struck his boat and almost capsized it. Pablo's head got smashed against a railing and he was swept overboard by high waves. He almost drowned before his men could rescue him. After that, his mind was never the same. Some people around here think he's crazy and others believe he has psychic powers. I don't know what to think, and I don't know why he keeps watching me."

"Then I believe I'll watch him watch you," Bill said. "And so will everyone else. There's something about him I don't like. Maybe you should have gotten rid of him right at the beginning."

We drove into the dirt parking lot at the marina. "Velvet, where's the best place to park?" Eric asked.

"Over there, near that dock. Our boat is tied about half way up," I pointed. "It's not too far and we can carry everything in one trip. Look for a twenty-one-and-a-half footer, white with blue trim. There's a diving platform and a walk-through at the stern. You can't miss it."

"What's the name of your boat?" Sandy asked.

"Satin Doll."

"Satin Doll?"

"Yes. When my mother and father were young they liked to dance at the grand ballrooms in New York, and their favorite song was a saxophone piece called SATIN DOLL. My mother was so tiny and pretty that ever since then, that's what Dad called her. When he bought this boat last Christmas, just before she died, he named it for her."

Bill pointed up the line of boats tied to the dock. "There it is. What a beauty!"

Lee, customarily reserved, was the first to reach the boat and admire its sleek lines and comfortable interior.

I stepped over the gunwale into the boat. "Come aboard and make yourselves at home. The ice box and sink are under the bow near the storage space and bunks. The bathroom, the head, is at the foot of the steps. Eric and Bill and Lee, will you crew the boat this time? Later, we ladies will drive and you can enjoy the ride."

When the food and blankets were stowed, Eric settled himself in the captain's chair and studied the instrument panel and controls. Bill stood at the windshield surveying the other boat traffic in the marina, and Lee held the rope, ready to cast off when Eric gave the order.

Sandy, Jade and I curled up on the soft, blue and white lounge seats, out of the way, and watched the men handle the boat. "All right, King Neptune," Sandy said, "we're ready. Show us your watery domain."

"Right! Cast off, Lee. Let's flee to the land of mermaids and sirens' calls."

Chapter 17.

"Let's cruise up the coast and I'll show you some of the places where we're going to dive," Eric said as he eased the SATIN DOLL out of the NO WAKE zone of the harbor and into open sea.

"Take a look off to your right when we go around the point of the peninsula. That's Punta Doble, known for good, shallow diving; we'll dive there one day. On your left out toward the sea, there's a reef where we want to dive, too. There are brilliant sea fans, and schools of reef fish like grouper, cabrilla, angelfish, and parrotfish. Sometimes the barracuda and yellowtail tuna can be seen, too."

We scanned the white sandy shore, the slope upward toward the fringe of desert greenery on the rolling hills, and above the hills, rugged mountains of solid rock.

"Up ahead, underwater, is Lalo Cave. Lots of colorful little fish there. And there's another cave nearby where we can catch crabs on the walls and dive for lobsters."

The scenery was dramatic and my mind stored each impression on its floppy disc to recall the next time I was stuck in a traffic jam. My interest, however, was divided between the terrain and my friends in the boat.

I watched Jade lean her head back on the cushion and inhale the sea air. Sunshine bathed her face, and sea breeze blew wisps of glossy, black hair loose from her French braid. "This is heavenly," she said. "I love the mountains of Colorado, but this is a whole other world."

Lee couldn't seem to take his eyes off her. Had he never seen Jade this happy? Was he wondering what it would take to keep her this way?

We cruised the coast for miles, exploring every bay and beach, looking into the crystal water at starfish and sand dollars, spiny puffer fish and stingrays.

"Eric, can we pull into shore and have our picnic over there?" I asked, pointing to a long, white arc of beach. "That's Algodones Beach and the water is lovely for a swim before lunch."

"You bet! We can go ashore anyplace along here. The beach drops off fairly rapidly and I don't see any submerged rocks. Maybe everyone would like to walk past that first sand dune to see Catch 22 Beach after we eat," Eric said.

We swam and splashed each other in water fights, then spread beach blankets on the sand and laid out our lunch to munch leisurely in the wonderful clear sunshine. I sure wouldn't be a very good mushroom; I couldn't stand a life without this sun.

We ate and teased and joked and laughed. Eric told some of his stories about dives in other seas. Contented, we lay on the warm sand and enjoyed each other and the shore.

Later, Jade sat up, studied the scenery, and said, "Velvet, look at all those palm trees growing up the side of that desert mountain. How do they get enough water to survive?"

"You can't tell it from here, but those palms are growing in a mountain canyon with a desert spring. It's hard to believe, I know, but it's a grassy oasis. And at the top of the canyon, in that limestone cliff, there's a cave with cool, sparkling water that cascades over the entrance and flows down the canyon, and tropical vines grow out of every crevice in the rocks. From the cave you can look over the crowns of the palm trees and all the way across the desert to the sea. It's one of the most beautiful views in this whole area, and hardly anyone knows about it, it's so secluded and hard to reach."

"Can we go see it?" Jade asked.

"Sure. Maybe tomorrow we can drive to the riding stable near the yacht club and rent horses. We can ride to the base of the mountain, but we'll have to climb the rest of the way on foot."

I looked around at the others in our group. "Does anybody else want to go?"

"No, thanks," Sandy declined. "I'd like to do a little painting."

"I think Bill and Lee and I ought to take the boat out and get some more experience handling it. Every boat has its own personality, you know," Eric said.

"Then we'll go exploring on our own, if you're sure you don't mind," I said.

Bill's dark expression told me he was not very enthusiastic about the idea. I put my arms around his neck and said, "We won't be gone more than four hours at the most. Besides, we'll leave a trail of tortilla crumbs for you to follow, just in case we're not back on time. You won't have any trouble finding us and rescuing us from the Wicked Witch of the Sonora Desert. And Pablo will be miles away. You go have a good time yourself, and don't worry about us. We'll be perfectly all right."

"You're sure?" Bill asked uneasily.

"I'm sure," I promised. "All we're going to do is explore an exotic, beautiful, hidden cave."

Chapter 18.

"Jade, I'm never going to remember all those details for diving. I listened to Eric's lecture yesterday afternoon and studied the dive manual all evening, but it doesn't soak in," I confided as we drove past the marina and around the edge of the bay to the riding stable.

"It's Greek to me, too," she consoled me. "I'm a mountain girl. A runner. I don't know anything about the ocean or the desert. But Sandy said everything will fall into place when we actually put on our wet suits and scuba gear and wade into the surf. You can trust whatever Sandy says."

"You seem to know her really well," I said.

"Yes, she was my art teacher, and she also sponsored the Cherry Creek High School Debate Team. We traveled all over the Rocky Mountain Region for competitions. My dad usually drove the van on our trips, and he says that next to my mother and my aunt, Sandy is the finest woman he's ever known. He thinks she's perfect for Eric and hopes they'll get married."

"That explains those affectionate gazes and relaxed conversations between them. They're not demonstrative, but they obviously feel a lot of affection for each other," I said.

"I don't mean to be too personal," I added, "but what about you and Lee?"

Jade turned in her seat and looked directly at me. She sighed. "I like him. I've liked him from the moment I stepped off the plane in Shanghai and he and his brother met us as our tour guides. But I don't know how he feels about me."

"Why not?" I asked. "I think his feelings are quite transparent."

"He's so restrained and quiet! He's not really shy, he just doesn't express his feelings. I know he's kind and understanding. Concerned. Good natured. Smart. He's determined to become a doctor. But where do I fit in?" Jade asked, bewildered.

"Have you ever asked him?" I asked.

"Me? Heavens no! I'd be afraid of embarrassing him. And I don't dare flirt with him, either, he's so serious about everything. How am I ever going to know?

"Let me think about it," I said. "After I get to know him better, maybe I'll have an idea."

We drove up to the riding stable and parked the car at the corral gate. "What kind of horse do you want, Jade?" I asked.

"Gentle. One that's smart enough to know what to do to keep me from falling off. I haven't ridden a horse since I was little and visited my uncle in the Jemez Mountains of northern New Mexico."A wiry Mexican cowboy met us at the corral with a cheery hello and asked how he could serve us.

"We'd like a couple of horses that are easy to handle and won't spook and throw us or run away."

"Yes, ma'am. You want this little pinto and that roan. They're as gentle as puppies. Where are you going to ride?"

"We want to ride up the shore to Catch 22 Beach, then up the old airstrip across the desert to the foot of the mountain. We're going to climb the canyon where the palm trees grow," I answered.

The cowboy nodded. "I know the place. How long will you be gone?"

"Maybe four hours. No more."

"Good. Let me raise these stirrups so you can reach them easy and you'll be all set," the cowboy said.

He led the horses to a wooden feed trough we could stand on. We placed our feet in the stirrups, swung into the saddles, pulled the reins and turned the horses toward the gate.

"Have a good ride," the cowboy said as we rode out of the corral. "Watch out for rattlesnakes."

On the trail across the beach, Jade pointed to several deteriorating stone structures ahead of us. "What are those buildings up there? They look as though they've been shot up or bombed."

"They have. That's the old movie set for Catch 22. Those stone houses and the tower are really just chicken wire and plaster of Paris. I'll show you," I answered.

We rode to the edge of the old movie set. "Part of the war scenes were filmed here. See the air strip? That's where the bombers landed and took off."

"Is the airstrip still in use?" Jade asked.

"No, after they finished filming the movie and went back to Hollywood, drug smugglers discovered the runway and used it for flying cocaine, heroin and marijuana into Mexico. This area is so remote they could fly in and out without detection by the authorities."

"Are smugglers still using the airstrip?"

"Not very often. The police caught on to the smuggling system and now they patrol it. And, the asphalt runway is breaking down and there are pot holes, so it's rather risky for planes to land or take off. Especially at night, and that's when they have the best cover. Then, too, with the mountain at one end of the airstrip and the sea at the other, a pilot has to be unusually good to begin with."

"Why would they even have to land?" Jade asked. "Can't they just pass over the airstrip and drop the drugs to partners on the ground?"

"Yes. And they do. But the police are on to them. Sometimes you'll see patrol cars bouncing across the desert in the daytime, and frequently at night."

"Isn't that a police car over there right now?" Jade pointed. "Between the beach and the mountain. Where that big saguaro cactus is. Do you think they might have found a drug drop today?"

"Maybe so. Let's go see," I said. I dug my heels into my horse's ribs. He broke into a run and I leaned low over his arching neck, tightened my knees against his sides and pumped the reins to urge him faster. Exhilarated by the wind in our hair and a mystery in the desert, we galloped over the blistering sand to the cluster of policemen with shovels in their hands.

Chapter 19.

High on a stony mountain overlooking the parched desert a shirtless man sprawled on a limestone boulder, as tan and still as the scaly lizard basking at his feet. The man raised eight-powered binoculars and sharpened the focus on two young women riding horses across the sandy wasteland toward a small knot of police officers digging a shallow trench in the sand.

A beady-eyed lizard examined the solitary man with the same intensity and caution as the man who studied the scene not far below.

From a distance, the man and lizard, perfectly camouflaged, blended into the graceless scenery, seemingly dormant in the heat.

Only they knew the speed at which they could react, and would, if the need arose. But at the moment, neither the man nor the lizard had anything to fear.

Chapter 20.

A hundred yards from the patrol car and the policemen, we reined the horses to a stop.

"They're digging a trench. I'll bet a plane dropped a load of drugs to a dealer on the ground and for some reason he couldn't transport them out of the area fast enough and had to bury the stuff and run. Maybe he planned to come back later," I speculated in my best mystery-story style.

"That's an awfully big trench they're digging," Jade said, puzzled. "It's too big for cocaine or heroin. It would take too much of it to fill a hole that size, but it's not big enough for marijuana, at least not enough to make it worth their trouble. Marijuana has a lot of bulk. If the dealer was in so much danger that he had to get away fast, why did he just happen to be carrying a shovel? How did he have enough time to dig a trench that large? And look! There's clothing in it."

I stood up in the stirrups so I could see into the trench. "Jade, I can't believe this! There's a body in that hole," I said, excited but hushed.

Torn between morbid curiosity and revulsion, we rode closer to the sandy grave. The policemen, their shirts soaked with sweat, pants and leather boots crusted with dirt, concentrated on their horrible job and paid no attention to us.

"Help me lift her out," one of the officers grunted. Gingerly, two of the men lifted the body by her shoulders while two more grasped the feet. They laid her reverently on a canvas sheet, her only protection from the vicious cactus spines.

"Murdered. Stabbed in the chest and stomach. The flesh is so torn it must have been done with a serrated knife," one of the policemen said.

"Yeah," the Chief of Police said. "Long blade. Wide. Like a diver's knife. And look at those punctures in her eyes. Whoever killed this girl is a sadist. Had to be insane. The coroner will find out whether the killer tortured her before he murdered her, or after. Don't matter much to the poor child now; either way, he killed her soul."

"Chief, don't you think it's too much of a coincidence, this body?" the tallest policeman asked. "Here's a young woman, seventeen, eighteen years old, maybe five feet tall, Anglo, dark hair. Doesn't she remind you of the one that washed up in the marina a couple or three weeks ago? And look over here. There are footprints all around the grave, and I bet they'd lead us to somebody or someplace we oughta know about."

"I saw them. Here's a good clear one. Several, in fact. The shoe soles are cut from rubber tires. Left sole says B. F. Good... Foot size about ten-and-a-half or eleven, I'd judge. We'll take casts of them and then get the body into town. I want to send a tracker with a dog and a posse of men to follow this killer. There's no telling where he might have gone. Coulda gone down to the beach and into a boat. Over to the airstrip and had a vehicle hid. Or even up one of these mountains to a hideout. There's no end of places to hole up. It's not much different now from when sea pirates and bandits terrorized everybody on this coast, and that wasn't too many years ago," the chief said.

Jade looked at me in alarm. "Let's go. This scares me," she whispered.

"Just a second," I said and slid off my horse.

"Excuse me, sir, but did you say you found a dead body in the marina?" I asked the Chief of Police.

He looked at me, annoyed at my boldness and interference. He started to tell me to leave. Then, for some reason, he changed his mind.

"Yes, ma'am. About three weeks ago. The body was in the water too long for the coroner to be sure of the cause of death, but the girl's head was smashed and something had punctured or eaten her eyes."

The chief seemed to be on the verge of saying more, hesitated, looked hard at me, at Jade, and back at me. He made up his mind then, and said, slowly and very distinctly so there would be no mistake in what we heard, "Two of you girls alone on the desert. Small. Anglo. Dark hair. Like these bodies we're finding. It wouldn't hurt for you to stay closer to home."

The warning was plenty clear. Was that why the chief didn't run us off earlier? Did he want us to learn about these vicious deaths so we'd be frightened? If he did, he was certainly successful.

"Velvet, please," Jade pleaded.

"Okay. I'm ready. We're going right now."

We rode in silence, shocked by the horror of the stab wounds and punctured eyes of the dead girl.

"I still can't believe it," I said. "This is not your typical high-crime district, you know. Nothing like it has ever happened here before."

Jade said philosophically, "But sometimes life serves up some terrible surprises."

I looked at the expression on her face and made a guess at what she was thinking: her own personal experience, the shocking attack in Beijing. "I have you to myself now, Jade. There's no one else around.

"When I'm in the city I'm always alert to possible danger and I'm careful about things like not going out at night alone and keeping my car doors locked, but this is a totally new experience," I said. "The beaches and hills and mountains of San Carlos were always so safe a woman could go anyplace alone. At least, they could 'til now. It would be terrible to think we couldn't be safe here anymore, free to come and go as we please.

"Jade, we're almost at the turn-off for the trail that winds up the canyon to the cave at the top of the cliff. Do you still want to see it? Actually, it's so peaceful and beautiful up there it might make us feel better before we go home."

"Yes, I'd like to see it. I'm not ready to face everyone anyway. This has me really shook up," Jade replied.

"Me, too," I confessed. "Maybe the climb to the cave will calm us before we have to tell Bill what we saw. I dread giving him something more to worry about and I already know what he's going to say. I can't stand to have another scene like the one the day he arrived, but sure as anything, if we don't tell him, someone else will. Someone at the marina or in town. And then he'll really be mad. It'll be better if he hears it from us first, don't you think?"

"Yes, it will," Jade agreed.

"Come on, let's go, then. The cave is sheltered and safe. We can duck under the waterfall and cool off before we ride back to the stable and drive home."

Chapter 21.

Heat waves shimmered above the sweltering desert sand. We urged our horses into a fast walk up the gentle, gradual rise toward the foot of the canyon. There wasn't any trail, but we could see the tops of palm trees in the oasis above us, and followed a dry, gravelly stream bed between rolling hills.

We gained altitude, left the prickly pear cactus and thorny bushes behind, and tall, green grass and shrubs took their place. Around the final, scorching foothill we entered a cool, shady paradise of Mexican fan palms and stately date trees, green fronds rustling in the breeze sweeping up from the sea. Small pools of clear water reflected lush grass.

"Here's where we dismount," I said and swung out of the saddle. "We can tie the horses to one of these palm trees where they'll have shade while we climb to the cave."

"How do we get there?" Jade asked, examining the rugged face of the steep, rocky mountain towering above.

"There's not really any trail until we get to the very top, but we can climb a dry streambed. We'll have to keep our eyes open, though. There are scorpions and tarantulas all over this mountain, and plenty of rattlesnakes, too. We mustn't break any rocks loose from the trail, either, 'cause they can start a rock slide."

I took the lead, walking carefully, placing my feet firmly on the slippery, loose sand and gravel.

The desert sun beat down, and half way up the mountain there was no more cool breeze to stir the clear air. Out of breath from the exertion and tropical temperature, we stopped to rest.

"Turn around and look at that view," I said. "You can see beyond the desert and across the Sea of Cortez practically all the way to Baja California. Isn't it spectacular? I love it here more than anyplace else I've been."

Jade surveyed the scene. "It compares with the infinite space in Colorado, our high mountain peaks that overlook great open plains and valleys. I don't know which I like better, the mountains or the sea. I guess what I treasure most is the sense of peace they both give me."

"Maybe you'll show me your mountains someday," I suggested and stood up to continue the trudge up the blistering cliff.

"Listen! I hear the waterfall," I said after another twenty minutes of climbing. "And look!"

Through the crowns of palm trees we caught a glimpse of the shady opening of the cave. Sparkling water cascaded off the limestone overhang and collected in clear, quiet pools, and lacy green vines clung to the cool, dark, rocky walls. "It's exquisite!" Jade gasped. "How can such a paradise exist in a desert mountain?"

"I don't know, but I think a geologist would. Come on. I'll show you the inside of my secret hideaway."

I took a couple of steps, got a clear, unbroken view of the cave, and stopped cold in my tracks. I threw my arms straight out to my sides to block Jade's path.

"Stop!" I whispered. "Don't move."

Startled, she stopped abruptly and looked around me into the shadowy cave.

"What's there? What do you see?"

As silently as possible I edged my way along the narrow path on the side of the cliff until I stood on the wide, flat, natural rocky platform at the opening of the cave. Jade cautiously crept up behind me.

"I thought you said hardly anyone knows about this place," she said, puzzled at what we saw.

"Shh. We'll look around. But we'll have to stay quiet. Do you hear anything?" I asked.

Slowly and silently we tiptoed closer. Then, alarmed and not comprehending what we were seeing, I grabbed Jade's arm.

A stone fire pit built in the center of the rocky entrance was filled with charred wood, evidence of many recent fires now dead and cold.

Several large, flat rocks served as primitive tables for smoke-blackened skillets and empty bottles and cans. Nearby, spread in the shade, was an army surplus sleeping bag. A few articles of dirty clothing, mostly jeans and shirts, and a pair of rubber tire-soled native sandals, lay scattered across the floor. "Someone is using this cave as a home," I murmured, dismayed.

"Whoever it is lives like a pig," Jade observed. "Their trash is everywhere. I wonder ..."

"Jade! Look! Look at what's here!" I whispered. "Knives. Guns. Gasoline. And sticks of dynamite. Quick! We've got to get out of here!"

Quietly, praying that no one saw us, we scurried out of the cave into the sunshine and the trail along the edge of the cliff to the dry stream bed we must climb down.

Jade started to ask, "What do you think..."

"Shh. Don't talk!" We stopped only long enough to scan the trail behind us and the streambed below to make sure no one was following or lying in wait. We saw no sign of anyone. We hurried down the mountain as fast as we could on the loose gravel, trying not to slip or turn an ankle. If we lost our footing, we'd have a long, hard slide with no bushes to grab to break our fall. Not to mention the cactuses and centipedes and rattlesnakes along the way.

Once we finally reached the foot of the mountain we were able to walk more safely and rapidly toward the palm oasis where our horses were tied.

We hurried around one final boulder blocking our view of the horses. The grassy oasis was only fifty feet ahead.

"Oh, no!" I groaned.

"What? What's wrong?"

"The horses. They're gone. This is where we tied them. See their hoof prints?"

"We must not have tied the reins well enough and they pulled loose," Jade said. "I'll bet they trotted back to the stable."

"No. They didn't get loose by themselves. They couldn't have. I'm certain of it. Somebody else was here. Somebody deliberately untied our horses and drove them away," I said, furious that anyone would pull a stunt like that.

"Velvet, look!" Jade screamed and pointed to the base of the palm tree where we had tied the horses. "Look there!"

We ran to the patch of grass now trampled flat by panicked hoofs. A mound of red and matted fur, long, black-tipped ears, and the broken legs of a jackrabbit now dead lay stretched and staked across the ground. Still-warm blood flowed from its slashed throat onto the moist dirt, and stiletto punctures mutilated its dull, still, amber eyes.

Chapter 22.

Jade and I knelt over the broken, bloody body of the rabbit. Nothing made any sense: this rabbit, the dead woman in the desert, someone living in the cave.

"Do you think it hopped under the horses and they stepped on it or kicked it to death?" Jade asked.

"No. This was a wild rabbit. It wouldn't hop under our horses even to feed on fresh grass. Look how the throat was slashed so cleanly. It was done with a knife, not a horse's hoof. See how all four of its legs are fractured? And notice the tiny punctures all around the eyes? This was no accident. It was a deliberate act of torture. Only a human being could inflict this kind of misery on the poor thing."

"I don't understand," Jade said.

"I don't either, but somebody murdered this rabbit and staked it where we'd be sure and find it. I think it was the same person who untied our horses and drove them away."

"But who would do such a thing? Do we even know anybody in Mexico who would have a reason?"

I thought about it. "Maybe we do know somebody. And maybe somebody knows we do. Did you notice all those footprints in the dirt? The ones the hoof prints didn't stamp out? Those prints were left by shoe soles made from rubber tires. That person killed the rabbit to warn us."

"To warn us? Of what? Hadn't we better get out of here?" Jade asked anxiously.

"Yes. As fast as we can."

Scared and shaking, we ran down the foothill toward the floor of the desert.

"It's hot!" Jade panted. "We shouldn't run any farther when it's so blistering. Let's rest for a few minutes and cool off. How far do you think it is to the riding stable?"

"Three miles, probably. But there's a dirt road not too far from here, and if we can get to it, maybe someone will come along in a car or truck and give us a ride," I said without much hope.

Tired and perspiring, we walked as fast as we could toward the rutted road which meandered through the desert, around cactuses and brambles, sometimes close to the seashore and other times near the foot of the mountains.

Waves of heat rose from the hot sand and distorted our vision so we couldn't be sure what we saw. The first car in the distance was merely a mirage.

"Velvet, what do you think is going on?" Jade asked in the ominous, silent desert.

"What do I think? I think it's very mysterious that our gardener Juan suddenly disappeared without a word and was never seen again. That a man I've never heard of showed up at our house at a time when I'd be there alone. That he was told to watch me, and does watch me all the time. And those rubber tire shoe soles he wears? They make the same kind of prints we saw around the grave in the desert and around the tortured rabbit. I think it's strange that nobody knows where Pablo lives, and all of a sudden somebody with an arsenal of weapons is living in a secluded cave with an unobstructed view of the desert, the airstrip and the coast. I think I'm scared out of my wits, is what I think."

"What are we going to do?" Jade asked. "Should we leave San Carlos and go back to the States?"

"I think we...Oh, look! See that cloud of dust? Somebody's driving up the road."

"Let's flag them down," Jade said and started to wave her arms.

"What if it's the murderer?" I cautioned her.

She groaned. "You're right. What if it is? Well, then, let's hide in the bushes 'til we can see who it is, and if they look okay we can step into the road. "

As quickly and furtively as skittish desert deer, we slipped between thorny bushes beside the ruts and crouched out of sight.

"Can you see anything?" Jade asked.

"Almost. As soon as they come around the next curve."

Tense and nervous, we listened to the drone of the motor and the groan of the vehicle as it eased over ruts and bumps, slowly coming closer in a storm of powder-fine dust.

"It's the van! It's Eric and Bill!" I screamed and leaped from our hiding place. I crashed through the brambles, caught my hair and clothes on wicked thorns, and jumped into the middle of the road to wave my arms. Jade clambered out of the brambles, too, waving frantically and yelling.

Eric braked sharply and Bill sprang from his door even before the van slid to a dusty stop. He ran to me and threw his arms around me, and Eric rushed to Jade like she was a long-lost little sister.

"What happened to you? Where've you been? We've been worried about you. You're two hours late. Your horses returned to the stable with empty saddles. What in the world happened to you?" Eric bombarded us.

Bill released me and stepped back an arm's length. His alert eyes darted from me to Jade and back to me, instantly seeing our fear. "You're scared, aren't you? Thirsty and tired, too. Something bad happened. Come get in the van. We'll take you home. You can tell us about it on the way."

Chapter 23.

The next morning Bill crumpled his napkin and placed it beside his breakfast plate. He pushed back his chair and crossed one foot over the other knee. "Today we're going to stay together. Eric, do you want to propose our plan?"

"Sure. You've learned all you need to know from the dive manuals and my instructions, and now you're ready to put on your diving gear and go into the water

"Really? We finally made it?" I asked.

"Really. Even you," Eric grinned.

"Thank heavens. I thought I'd never get the hang of inspecting each piece of equipment, putting it together and taking it apart, and getting it on right. I am sure of all the underwater communication signals, though," I said.

"That's because you can't stand it if you can't talk, right?" Eric teased.

"Surely, sir, I speak not too much nor too long," I retorted indignantly.

It was a great relief and comfort to be with my friends. By the time Jade and I told them about the things which happened on our horseback ride yesterday I had such a surge of tension that

I felt as though my circuit breaker had kicked off and left me with no energy at all.

I expected Bill to be angry, but he wasn't. On the contrary, he was genuinely sympathetic.

Eric thought we should tell the police about the dead rabbit, the horses untied and driven away, someone living in the cave, and my suspicion of Pablo even though I didn't know any reason why he'd threaten us. But Bill said no. From a legal point of view, they weren't grounds for a case. Bizarre and scary, yes.

Illegal, no. Bill and Eric didn't think there was any real risk, no need to go home. At least not now.

We agreed to stick close together, but if one of us wanted to do something else any time, another person would go along. No one would go anyplace alone, and we'd make sure we knew where everyone was at all times.

My night was filled with bad dreams, but today was a new day. A new adventure. I was up for it.

"What are you going to teach us next?" I asked.

"You're going to work in the water with your mask, regulator, mouthpiece, air hose, buoyancy compensator, weight belts and air tanks today. You'll learn to make a proper entrance and exit from land, and Algodones will be an ideal beach to use. Today or tomorrow you're also going to learn to buddy breathe," Eric said.

"Buddy breathe? Is that like mouth-to-mouth resuscitation, or is it some kind of soul kiss?" I asked in all innocence. After all...

Jade giggled. Lee looked puzzled. Sandy rolled her eyes upward and sighed her "Oh my" sigh.

Eric struggled to keep a straight face, although I didn't know why. "No, Velvet, buddy breathing is not a soul kiss."

Maybe not, but it sounded pretty exotic to me.

Eric chose to ignore me and got back to his instructions. "We'll be working as partners. I'd like you to choose your partners now."

Sandy immediately turned to Bill and said, "Will you buddy with me?" That surprised me. I thought I'd get to be his buddy.

Sandy saw my disappointment and assured me, "After everyone has the buddy breathing technique down pat, we'll change partners again."

That made me feel a little better. I suppose it was actually better for Bill to learn from someone who knew what she was doing.

"Velvet, I want you to be my partner, okay?" Eric asked.

"Okay. Lessons from the head honcho himself."

So, Jade and Lee ended up as buddies to each other. That was going to be interesting.

"Any questions? No? Then let's load the gear and pack a picnic lunch," Eric said.

Maria laid out the picnic supplies, food and cold drinks. Lee brought the ice chests from the storage room and he and Jade packed them while Bill collected the beach blankets and towels and carried them to the van.

When everything was loaded, I asked Eric what we should wear for our first diving lesson.

"Just throw a windbreaker over your swimsuit in case you get chilly when we're boating or when we finish diving." It certainly didn't take us long to get ready. Only Zip-Lock was faster.

Eric drove the van to the parking lot at the marina, found a space near the dock, and parked. "Okay, here we are. If we can't carry everything to the boat in one trip, Lee and I'll come back. Would you store everything where it won't move around? Make sure the life vests are where they're quick and easy to reach," Eric said.

The men began handing the gear out of the van, and we each carried a load to the boat. There was such an air of exuberance that none of us could stop chattering. We were actually going to work in the water!

I already had an idea of the varieties of fish and plants we'd see underwater, since I'd watched fishermen bring their day's catch to the pier, but actually to see the fish alive in their own habitat was so exciting I could hardly stand it. Get ready, Monsieur Cousteau. You're going to have a whole new crew.

Chapter 24.

An old tan Ford sedan with a rusty dent in the left front fender followed their van at a discreet distance from the top of the peninsula, down the hill to the marina.

The driver parked between yachts and trailers hauled up beside the repair shop. Car motor still running, he watched the divers unload their van, lock it and carry their gear to the SATIN DOLL.

When the divers' backs were to the repair shop the Ford rolled slowly, quietly, to the center of the parking lot, raising no dust, no notice.

Muscles tense in his bare shoulders, the driver parked between a large motor home and a pickup truck.

He lit a cigarette with a wooden kitchen match, waved the flame out and threw the match into the otherwise clean parking lot.

Looking through and beyond the windows of the pickup shielding him from the divers' view, he waited until the SATIN DOLL cast off and merged with other boats easing out of the bay toward open sea.

When the SATIN DOLL passed the last buoy, the pilot of the boat opened the throttle wide until the boat was planing sleekly over the glassy sea. Its course was definitely north and west, hugging the coast.

With a nod of certainty, the man in the Ford sedan threw his burning cigarette out the window and started the motor. Hurriedly, he drove out of the parking lot and turned onto a dirt road which wound along the bay, around the edge of the lagoon, through the dusty desert and beside the coast to the best beaches for scuba divers. The best one of all was Algodones. The man smiled.

Chapter 25.

"The first thing we're going to do is place our dive flag on the water where we're going to work so other boaters will know we're down there," Eric said after we unloaded our equipment on Algodones Beach.

"Next," he continued, "you need to put on your protective dive clothing. Sandy and I will help you with your buoyancy control device and weight belt. You already know the principal of water displacement, and this exercise will simply be a matter of using that principal."

We took our time putting on our wet suits and equipment, meticulous about doing everything right. Sandy and Eric continuously checked each of us to make sure we had no questions or mistakes.

"Okay, now your masks, regulators, hoses and tanks. You've practiced using them on dry land numbers of times, but we'll help you this time anyway because it will be somewhat different when you enter the water," Eric said.

When I was ready I asked Eric for a final inspection. He examined every fitting. "Fine. You're set. As soon as the others are ready, we'll walk backwards into the sea. I'll lead, the class will fan out behind me and do what I do, and Sandy will follow. Watch us," he directed.

"We look like an aerobics class from outer space with these wild, neon colors of wet suits, masks and fins," Jade laughed. "We're going to give the tropical fish plenty of competition."

Sandy agreed. "Yes, and that's not all bad. You'll practically glow in the dark and it'll be easy to see you underwater. Anyone will be able to find you if you get separated from your buddy. Which you are NOT supposed to do," she added firmly. She wasn't a high-school teacher for nothing.

"Ready?" Eric asked. We nodded yes. Our masks and hoses nodded with us. "Then turn around with your back to the sea. Watch your step and watch Sandy and me. Walk backwards into the water until I tell you to stop. The tide is out and there's no surf, so you're not going to bounce around. You'll just float when you're deep enough. This time, we won't go any deeper than where you can touch the floor of the sea. Any questions?"

"Yes," Jade said. "Once we're deep enough to float, what are we going to do?"

"Sandy and I will check your buoyancy and give you some practice in altering it. We'll make sure you're equalizing the pressure in your body properly and breathing evenly. We'll also make sure you can clear your mask if it gets water in it."

"Any buddy breathing?" I asked. I wanted to watch Jade and Lee as partners.

"Not today, sorry. We'll work on these other skills until you're comfortable with them. Maybe tomorrow we'll buddy breathe," Eric answered. "Okay? Then let's turn our backs to the sea and waddle in."

Chapter 26.

Algodones Beach, a mile-long arc of snowy-white sand, curved toward the northwest and ended in an outcropping of volcanic rock and a jumble of rough, red boulders which long ago had fractured from it and tumbled into the clear aqua sea.

Tidal pools sparkled in the bright sunshine. Blue damselfish and yellow and blue striped angel-fish flitted in seaweed waving in the crystal current. Fringed sea anemones, spiny sea urchins and cone-shaped limpets clung to the wet craggy rocks.

A man in frayed cotton twill shorts and native sandals climbed up the rocky outcropping and searched for a suitable place to sit. A place where he could see without being seen.

Finding the right spot, a large boulder worn smooth from eons of wind and surf, he sat down and dangled his stocky legs over the side.

Letting the tropical sun beat down on his well-browned, bare shoulders, he lifted powerful binoculars to his eyes.

Searching through the lenses, he located the scuba divers moving duck-like into Algodones Bay. He fiddled with the focus. Frowned.

How could he be sure who was wearing those masks and diving suits? Two of the women were short enough, all right, but they both had long, dark hair. Which one was the right one? Or weren't either of them the right one? Why did so many women look alike? Until too late?

Would he have to watch and wait until they finished their diving lesson and came out of the water? After they got out of that scuba gear, would he be able to know for sure?

Silently, he settled down to wait.

Seagulls, boobies and frigates which scattered when the man first arrived now resumed their patient pattern of circles in the sky, black, beady eyes seeing every piscine movement in the sea. Detecting their prey, they plummeted, screaming, into the water and seized silvery fish flashing in the morning sunshine, fish too innocent, too oblivious of danger to flee.

The man studied them, admired their hunting skill, compared their life to his own. Circle and watch, select your prey, plunge.

He shifted his binoculars to a diving flag anchored in Algodones Bay.

Chapter 27.

"You did well," Eric congratulated us. "Let's quit for today. It would be counterproductive to overdo it."

We removed our gear and loaded it into the boat. "We'll rinse it in clear water after we get home," Bill said.

"How about lunch now?" Sandy asked.

We spread beach blankets on the sand and opened the ice chests.

"A feast!" Bill exclaimed. "We'll soon be so fat we'll make good shark food." It would take more than a picnic lunch to put fat on Bill's trim, strong build.

We made beach nachos with chunks of cold chicken, cheese and salsa on crisp tostados, and ate them with pasta salad, mangoes and papayas, and chilled juices.

Full, warm and happy, we slathered sunscreen on our bodies and stretched out in the sun, lazy and happy with friends.

"Anybody want to ski on the way back to the marina?" Eric asked later when we began to stir.

"Sure! I do!" I said promptly. "I never turn down a chance to waterski. It's an absolute passion of mine. Sandy, do you want to ski, too?"

"Yes, and if Bill will drive, Eric and I can ski double."

"Be glad to," Bill said. "And I'll take a turn after you've skied all you want."

"Lee? Jade?" Eric asked.

Lee shook his head. "No, sorry. Never learned in Shanghai."

"I don't know how, either," Jade said, "but I'd like to learn some time."

"Great! We'll teach both of you tomorrow. Okay?"

"Yes, but it might take a while. You'll probably have to drag me half way to the Pacific Ocean before I learn to stay on my feet."

"That's fine. We can use you as bait and troll for marlin," Eric teased. "I've wanted to land a trophy fish for a long time and now's my chance."

"Huh! Try explaining that to my dad," Jade retorted sassily. "Or mine," I added. "You know how it is with fathers and their only child."

Bill listened and scowled. Why did he always lose his sense of humor whenever I mentioned my father? What was eating him, anyway? Would I never understand men?

Chapter 28.

"Lee, if you'll bring the garden hose from the storage room, we can connect it over here and wash our equipment," I said when we finished unloading the van.

"Be sure and get all the salt out of everything," Eric cautioned. "We'll dry the equipment and wetsuits in the shade. Sun and salt aren't too good for this kind of gear."

Working together we washed everything including us, thanks to our water fights. We were soggy by the time we laid our gear out to dry any needed to lay ourselves out, too.

Sandy said, "I have a suggestion. After we get dried and dressed, let me take you to the cantina for an enchilada supper. I hear there's a great guitarist after seven o'clock."

"Sold!" Eric accepted.

"Is seven okay with everyone? The sun will be behind the mountains by then and there'll be a cool evening breeze."

"Seven it is," we all agreed.

The cantina was a red brick restaurant with a hand-laid flagstone terrace on the beach. Part of the red tile roof was open to the stars, part was covered with palm fronds that rustled in the gentle sea breeze.

"I propose that we eat dinner out here in the open," Sandy said and led us to the terrace. "After we eat, we can go into the bar and listen to the guitarist."

A waiter in a tropical shirt and white twill shorts led us to a large table with a decorated leather top.

"Allow me," Bill said and pulled a chair out for me. Eric and Lee seated Sandy and Jade, and the waiter brought a glowing hurricane lamp.

"Jade, what do you suggest?" Lee asked, looking at the Mexican menu. "Do they make duck fajitas here like we ate at the 'Sick Duck' Restaurant in Beijing?"

Jade laughed. "No, but I bet you can get a chicken fajita. About the only thing you'll find here that you ate in China is shark fin soup. One thing I'm sure of is this Mexican meal won't be as strange as that first dinner you took us to at the family restaurant in Shanghai."

"Idea," Eric interrupted. "Let's order a little of everything and Lee can experiment to find out what he likes. Next time he can specialize."

"Swell. Why don't we start with chili con queso, guacamole salad and tostados," Sandy said. That was generous, since she was picking up the check.Half way through dinner, Lee took a bite of spicy carne adovada, then a long drink of icy water.

"Too hot?" Jade asked.

"Yes, but I'll get used to it. It's no worse than some of our Oriental peppers. We just spread ours out a little more," he said, his eyes tearing.

At the end of supper, the waiter took us to the small bar open to a sky so full of stars they looked like silver glitter sprinkled on black velvet.

He seated us in comfortable leather chairs in a semi-circle around the guitarist.

"Welcome to the cantina. What may I play for you?" the slender, sleek-haired young man asked.

With a wordless glance, Sandy sent a message to Eric. Understanding, Eric asked the guitarist, "Do you know an old song, *Cuando Caliente Del Sol?*"

"Certainly," the musician said. He strummed his mellow guitar, and with a smile in his eyes, crooned romantically to Sandy and Eric.

"How about *La Bamba*?" I asked next.

"Yes, and you must dance," the guitarist said.

"Me?"

Sandy added, "Yes, you. Go on. You, too, Bill."

A few beats later everyone was dancing on the tiny postage-stamp dance floor.

Even Lee. Lee might be serious and reserved some places he went, but he was certainly no slouch on the dance floor. Where had he learned to dance like that? In the People's Republic of China? Clearly, I was going to have to revise my understanding of China.

The guitarist slowed the tempo so we could dance close. The men each danced with all of us. That was nice. A feeling of group adhesion: we all belonged to one another. It made me feel safe and secure.

When the guitarist stopped for a break, Eric said to Bill, "Your turn. How about sitting down at the piano and playing for us?"

Bill plays the piano? I didn't know that. He'd never mentioned it to me.

Entirely at ease, Bill took a seat at the bench and ran his long fingers up and down the keyboard in a few soft arpeggios, getting the feel of the piano. He turned to us and asked, "What would you like to hear?"

Without hesitating, Lee said, "Can you play "Sergei Rachmaninoff's *Prelude in C-Sharp Minor*?"

Bill nodded and bent over the keys, his wrists bent, hands suspended. Then, he dropped them onto the keys and struck the powerful, distinctive chords of the prelude followed by its softer, melodic notes.

Jade's mouth dropped open and her eyebrows lifted in surprise. Apparently, she didn't know Lee had any background in classical music, just as I didn't know about Bill. What other hidden talents were we going to discover in these men?

We listened, spellbound, to the end.

"Thank you, Bill. That was extraordinary," Lee said appreciatively.

"What now?" Bill asked.

"Do you know an old song my mother liked? *Ebb Tide*," I asked.

Bill's hands moved across the keys and played the lovely haunting melody my mother and father liked to dance to right here in this cantina. I could see them, Mother's head on Dad's shoulder, his arms holding her, moving to the rhythm. My eyes misty, I tried not to cry at the memory.

"Enough music," Bill said, sensitive to the change in my mood. "The diving boss said no late parties. It's time to go home."

"Sandy, I've had a wonderful evening. Thank you," I said, reluctant for it to end.

"I'm glad. So did I. And what's to stop us from doing it again?"

Chapter 29.

Behind the van, a rusty Ford sedan ground quietly up the hill, moved slowly, its lights off. It stayed close enough to the van to keep it within sight, far enough back not to be seen.

Eric's van slowed, turned into the Shepards' driveway, and stopped in the carport. Bill opened the door, dropped to the ground, and turned to hold out his hand for each of the women to descend.

A hundred yards away, the Ford stopped, idled, waited. The driver squinted his eyes; he tried to see more clearly each person who walked across the concrete floor and into the house.

"Can't tell!" He whammed the steering wheel angrily with his fist.

In the silence of the desert night he heard the front door close and the lock click. Yard lights, front and back, turned off. Another opportunity was lost.

Swearing under his breath, the man eased his car past the house and down the peninsula toward the road to the mountain cave.

Chapter 30

"Everybody ready?" Eric asked on Algodones Beach. "We'll go through the same drill this morning that we went through yesterday. Probably several times. Then we'll come out of the water, take a break and warm up.

"Today will we learn to buddy breathe?" I asked.

"Yes, today we'll buddy breathe," Eric laughed. "You're going to be my buddy today and the penalty for not passing the test is death by drowning."

I shot daggers at him, but with a diver's mask over my eyes, they were wasted. Another time...

We waded backwards into the water and began our drill. As nearly as I could tell, all of us had it down pat; nevertheless, we went through the whole routine four times before Eric signaled us ashore.

"You're doing terrific!" he applauded us. I tried to bow, but the weight of my tanks toppled me off balance. I did grin proudly behind my mask.

We took off our tanks and other gear and lay on the warm sand.

Just as we became drowsy, Eric suddenly leaped up, planted himself right in front of us, his legs straddled and arms widespread like a nightclub entertainer leaping onto a stage. And just as startling.

"Ladies and chentlemun, may I have your atten-shun? Eet ees time for zee main attrac-shun: zee buddy-breathe It gifs me much pleasure to dedee-cate zees performance to our own Velvet Shepard."

He did get our atten-shun.

"Now." He changed from showman to instructor like an ON-OFF switch on the wall. "You already learned that the buddy system adds to a diver's safety. A buddy becomes his extra set of eyes and ears and arms. Besides, diving is more fun when you share it with someone."

There was no question. We were having a great time

"You learned what to do if you run out of air for any reason. You practiced making a controlled emergency swimming ascent, exhaling all the way to the surface."

Heads nodded.

"You practiced no-mask swimming underwater for fifty feet. You know how to use your buddy's alternate air source . Those are the methods we prefer you use if you have an air shortage."

Eric paused, bent one elbow, stiffened his hand, and drew it toward his chest and throat, somewhat like a karate chop.

"What does this hand signal mean?"

"Out of air," Lee said.

"Right. And this?"

He cupped his hand and drew it toward his mouth.

"Buddy breathe. Share air," Jade responded.

"Correct. Buddy breathing is a little more complex than the other options, but once in a while a diver needs to use it. That might happen if you're deeper than forty feet, too deep to make a controlled emergency swimming ascent, and you're close to your buddy but he has no alternative air source. Am I making myself understood?"

Yes, we nodded.

"Okay. Let's put on all our equipment, go into the water, and learn to buddy breathe."

Eric and Sandy demonstrated the technique first, then talked us through it while we followed their instructions.

With Eric as my buddy you'd think I'd learn the breathing technique quickly and easily, but I couldn't seem to get the hang of it. Eric would breathe from the mouthpiece while I held my breath underwater, but when he'd pass the mouthpiece to me to inhale air while he held his breath, I'd inevitably turn it upside down or exhale instead of inhale or forget entirely what to do. I even dropped the blamed thing once, panicked, and clawed my way to the surface, the worst thing a diver can do.

"I'm sorry, Eric. I just can't do it," I apologized.

"Yes you can. Here. Practice with me above water, and we'll gradually sink lower as you get used to it."

I finally got it right. Half drowned but delirious with relief, I swam ashore with Eric's blessing. Everybody else was already sitting on the sand drinking cold pop, waiting for us to surface.

"Well, look what's finally dragging itself out of the sea. Let's hear it for Velvet!" Bill yelled and my friends cheered. I felt like a world-class winner receiving an Olympic Gold. Maybe an Olympic Lead was more appropriate in this case.

"Tomorrow, you'll change buddies and practice until it's second nature to you. After that, you'll have your test dives and qualify for certification. Then, San Pedro Island, here we come!" Eric promised.

That's what we came for and we were about to reach our goal: open-water scuba certification. What a thrill! I wished Dad were here.

Chapter 31.

At the far end of Algodones Beach, a dented, rusty, Ford again parked behind a lava outcropping, out of sight of the scuba divers.

A man with sun-browned, powerful shoulders sat on the lookout point and dangled his husky legs. He trained binoculars on two dark-haired women diving in the bay.

He wondered: *how many more days will they be concealed by those damn masks and other gear? When will I get a clear view? Be sure which one it is? Could I see them better from a boat in the bay?*

Get closer to them without them paying attention? Should I take the risk or not?

How much longer do I have to wait for my revenge?

He stilled his fury and impatience.

Waited.

Watched.

Chapter 32.

"This is our final day of class," Eric stated. "We're going to practice water rescues, mouth-to-mouth resuscitation and first-aid. You'll demonstrate that you know the underwater signals divers use for communication. And, you'll take your final diving exam."

Jade whispered to me, "Do you think everyone will earn their certification today?"

I nodded. No one but me had had difficulty, and I felt confident now that I could handle any situation that might arise. It had helped me that Eric was a patient instructor and that everyone else had encouraged me.

Eric continued his announcements. "When we finish, how about if we teach Jade and Lee to water ski?"

Lee, less reserved every day, locked his fists together, raised them over his head like a boxer in the ring and grinned, "I'm ready!"

"And then, tonight I'd like for you to be my guests for dinner at the Playa de Cortez on Bahía Bocochibampo. You can dress up, and we'll go over by boat instead of highway. It'll take about an hour each way, but the weather's fine and the moon is full."

"What's the Playa de Cortez?" Sandy asked.

I explained, "It's the most famous old, historic, Spanish Colonial hotel in this part of Mexico. The architecture is typical of the Colonial era. The dining terrace is in a citrus grove on the shore. For atmosphere, food and service, it's the best. Dad always took Mother and me there for dinner on Christmas Eve before we walked in the candlelight procession to the cathedral for midnight services."

This would be a big day and night, and we were especially eager to get to Algodones Beach to begin our final class and test.

Throughout the morning, no one had any problems with the water rescues, hand signals or first aid. All of us who went to China last year learned mouth-to-mouth before we went. Lee's father, a physician in Shanghai, had taught him, and Bill andI had learned in school.

We finished class, put on our diving gear and entered the water for our final exam.

"Congratulations, each of you," Eric said when we finished, surfaced and came ashore. "You have met the requirements to certify as open-water divers, and when you receive your certification cards you'll have full access to scuba equipment and air tanks at dive shops anyplace."

"Are we ready for a real dive?" Jade asked.

"Yes, I have every confidence that you know everything you need to know in order to dive safely and successfully and have fun doing it."

"Then, can we stow the scuba gear and get out the waterskis, now?" I asked. "I can hardly wait for Jade and Lee to learn my very most favorite sport."

"Yes, this is a good time. Who wants to be their instructor?"

"Bill, why don't you?" I asked. "You grew up in Minnesota with ten thousand lakes. You probably know more about boating and skiing than any of us."

"Be glad to," he replied. "Jade, would you like to learn first? Velvet and I'll show you how."

"I'd love it. What do I do?" she asked.

Chapter 33.

"Okay. Here's what I suggest," Bill said. "Velvet and I'll stay on the shore to show Jade and Lee what to do. Eric, why don't you drive the boat, and Sandy, you be the spotter to read our hand signals and tell Eric what's happening."

"Sure. Sounds good," Eric and Sandy agreed and waded to the boat floating peacefully a few yards out in the bay. They attached the ski rope to the ski bar on the back of the boat and threw the handles to us.

"Jade, you're first. Step into these foot pads and let me adjust them to fit," Bill said and laid the skis on the sand. "That's good. Here's your ski belt. It'll keep you afloat if you take a spill." He fastened it around Jade's little waist.

"I'll carry the skis into the water," I offered. "Let's wade out until you're about shoulder deep."

Lee waded with Jade, Bill and me, listening, watching, learning.

"Now," Bill directed, "take hold of this ski and slip your foot into the foot piece. Yes, that's right. Now this one. Let yourself float. Bend forward."

The boat was idling, its bow out to sea. Eric and Sandy watched and waited for our signal to start.

"Here's the tow handle. Grasp it firmly with both hands. Hold it straight ahead of you, horizontally, like this. Lean back in the water a tiny bit. Good. Bend your knees and bring your ski tips out of the water and hold them perpendicular to the horizon. Yes, that's right. Just relax. Try to hold that position. When you feel ready, yell, 'Hit it!' Eric will accelerate until the boat is planing. As it picks up speed, let the force of the water and the pull of the rope lift you out of the water and onto the surface."

"What if I fall?" Jade asked anxiously.

"Drop the tow handle immediately and float. Sandy will be watching and they'll circle around to bring the rope back to you. If your skis pop off, they won't go anywhere. You can swim to them easily."

"One more instruction," I added. "If you want to ski faster, make a fist with your thumb sticking up and raise your arm so Sandy can see you clearly. If you want to ski slower, point your thumb down."

"And stop?" Jade asked.

"Run your hand across your throat as though you're cutting it, and Eric will cut the motor."

"You're expecting an awful lot," she said.

"You can do it," Lee encouraged. "Anybody who can win the Bolder-Boulder 10K Run and race on the crumbled stones of the Great Wall of China can learn to water ski."

"That's right. Just start out pretending your feet are pushing against a brick wall and before you know it, you'll be skiing," I said.

"All right, I think I'm ready." Jade tightened her grip on the handle. "Hit it!" she yelled.

The stern of the boat dug into the sea as Eric pushed the throttle. Jade waggled unsteadily at first, but as the boat picked up speed she steadied herself and began to rise onto the surface of the sea.

"She's up!" Lee yelled. "She did it the first try!"

At the very moment we were sure Jade had the hang of it, she lost her balance. Legs, arms and skis flew every which way, and she crashed into the water with a great splash.

Jade came back up with a surprised look on her face, sputtered, wiped the water out of her eyes, and swam to collect her skis.

"Did you like it?" we asked when Eric and Sandy brought her back to shore.

"Yes, I want to go again, but let Lee try it first. I want to see how he does."

The three of us prepared Lee for his initiation and he went sailing over the water as easily as if he'd been born to ski.

"He has strength and coordination," Bill said to Jade. "And so do you. You'll be a good skier. Just give it another try or two."

"Do you know what made me fall?" Jade asked.

"No. Did you stub your toe?"

She shook her head. "Did you see that little aluminum fishing boat out in the bay?"

We hadn't noticed it, we were so intent on watching Jade.

"Well, there was one. When I skied toward it, I only had a few seconds to look—we were going so fast and we weren't that close, anyway—but I noticed a man was just sitting in the hot sun, no shirt, no hat, not fishing or anything. Just watching me with binoculars."

"That's really not too unusual," I said. "Lots of people like to watch skiers."

"Yes, but what I didn't understand was that at the moment I skied past him, he looked straight at me and drew his hand across his throat like he was cutting it. I thought he was trying to tell me something like maybe I was supposed to stop. When I let go of one ski handle and signaled Sandy to have Eric cut the motor, I lost my balance and fell. The next time I looked up, the boat and the man were gone."

Jade's brow crinkled in a question. "What was he trying to tell me? What did he mean when he slashed his throat? What did he want me to do?"

Chapter 34.

The men, wearing suits and ties, were sitting around the wrought-iron table on the terrace when we finished dressing for dinner.

"Would you look at these beauties!" Bill exclaimed. "How can three women who've marinated in brine all day become such a vision of loveliness?"

The men stood to offer their chairs. "Let's not sit," I said, eager for the cruise across the sea to Bocochibampo Bay and the hotel. "And let's drive our car instead of your van to the marina."

Sandy placed her arm through Eric's. "If you handsome hunks are ready, would you care to squire us to dinner?"

"It would be our greatest pleasure," Eric said.

Lee took Jade's hand in his, his first show of affection. Lo! Their romance was warming up.

We drove to the marina, parked, and walked out the dock to the SATIN DOLL. The men helped us board and we settled comfortably in the lounge seats, content to let the men crew the boat. Our high heels and dinner dresses were actually quite ridiculous in a motor boat, but we didn't care. It was fun.

Eric pushed a cassette into the stereo player and beautiful music drifted across the bay.

"We're ready. Will someone cast off? I figure it'll take us about an hour to get there. We can watch the sun set on the way," Eric said. He eased the boat out of the slip and into the channel.

Relaxed and happy during the trip, we sang along with the music and talked about scuba-diving trips we wanted to take. The sun dipped to the horizon, and in awe and silence we watched the aqua blue sea change to dazzling gold, and the purple of the mountain peaks towering over the brown desert turned red and lavender and pink. One of Mexico's famous sunsets that I love.

"Straight ahead, on the shore. That's the Playa," Eric said and pointed to the large colonial building shaded by trees of fire, swaying palms, bougainvilleas, hibiscus with bright tropical blossoms, and oleanders growing in perfectly manicured lawns and hedges.

"That's the citrus garden on the shore, there where the lanterns are swinging in the trees. The dining terrace is in that garden. Bill or Lee, will you take the line and tie us to the dock?"

We brushed the wind out of our hair, tossed our windbreakers onto the bunks inside the bow and stepped onto the flagstone dock where a mariachi band played.

"Jade, Lee, have you heard mariachis before?" I asked as the musicians moved toward us and began to play and sing *La Golandrina*.

"Never," said Lee. "Not in Denver, not in Shanghai. Never have I seen costumes like that, either. They're as spectacular as our embroidered royal silk robes."

He studied the black, tailored, waist-length coats trimmed with gleaming sterling silver buttons, and skin-tight pants with triple rows of sterling buttons down the sides from thigh to foot. The white shirts were ruffled, and the men wore red cummerbunds and ties. Their enormous felt hats were embroidered with silver stitchery and trimmed with sequins that glittered in the golden glow of the lanterns.

A smiling maître d' led us to our table beside the garden dance floor. The mariachis followed, formed a semi-circle in front of us, and played the opening bars of *Malaguena.*

"We are playing just for you," the leader of the band said. "We wish you a fine dinner, and later, we will play for you to dance. To good health." He pretended to raise a glass.

"To good health. And a long life," we responded

"Yes. Especially to a long life."

Chapter 35.

"I'm so full I'll sink when we dive tomorrow," Sandy said at the end of dinner.

"Me, too. Forget the weight belt," Jade agreed "I won't need one."

While the mariachis were on break, we lingered over coffee, and a delicate pink blossom floated into my cup. We listened to the waves gently slapping the shore and palm fronds rustling in the ocean breeze. Silver moonlight cast shadows on the grass and pearlized Sandy's and Jade's pale skin.

"How would you like to take a diving trip tomorrow?" Eric asked. "Go to San Pedro Island?"

"We'd like it a lot," Bill answered. "Where is it?"

"West/northwest from San Carlos Bay about 19 miles out to sea. Toward the Baja Peninsula."

"What makes it special?" Sandy asked.

"It's a large island entirely rock. A large colony of seals lives there and we'll see bulls and cows and pups all over the rocks and in the water. They aren't afraid of people so we'll be able to observe them closely."

While I listened, I noticed Lee's eyes gleaming. I wondered, was that from the plans for a diving trip, or was it from his dancing with Jade? They seemed more outgoing and affectionate all the time, and I thought it was great. However, Jade had told me she really was unable to fathom what Lee's feelings for her might be, and she was not jumping to any conclusions and neither should I.

"What time should we be ready?" Sandy asked. "How long will we be gone?"

"We should plan to be away a full day. We'll need to pack a lunch. Can everyone be ready by eight in the morning?"

"No problem," Sandy answered. "Fine with me," the rest of us said.

"Then why don't we have another dance or two and start home? It's getting late," Bill said.

"Good idea," Eric agreed. "When we get to the marina I want to fuel the boat and check it. Lee, will you help me? We'll put the life preservers in the bow where they'll be out of the nighttime dew, and get the diving flags and flares ready for tomorrow."

"Be glad to," Lee replied."While you do that, I'll take the ladies home and drive back for you," Bill said.

"And we can put together a lunch and have it ready," I suggested to Sandy and Jade.

The mariachis returned and enchanted us with their Mexican love songs that filled the warm, moist ocean night.

"Jade? One more dance before we leave?" Lee stood and offered his hand. Jade walked with him to the dance floor.

Sandy excused herself briefly and while she was gone Bill and Eric and I listened to the music and watched couples dance in the moonlight.

I just happened to glance at the table on my right at the far edge of the citrus garden and saw a man sitting in the shadows watching us. There was nothing strange about that and my eyes moved on to something else, but then it struck me that the man seemed somehow familiar. I did a double-take. Yes, I was almost sure of it.

I turned to Eric and whispered, "Eric, don't turn around now, but when you can without being obvious, look at the man at the table to your left, back in the shadows of the orange trees. He reminds me of that guy who roared past our driveway and raised all the dust the first day we were here."

In a few moments Sandy returned. Eric stood to escort her to the dance floor and also have an excuse to look at the man I was curious about. He casually surveyed the entire garden, then looked back at me.

"Which table, Velvet?" he asked. "I don't see anyone."

The man had disappeared so quickly and quietly we hadn't even see him leave.

Had he been aware we were talking about him? Had he really been watching us? Or was he only watching one of us? Which one? What was he trying to see or find out? Why did he leave so abruptly? Why did he always disappear the moment we spotted him?

I was curious, and still mad from all the dust the guy stirred up, but I wasn't afraid. It certainly wasn't anything to go to the police about: a guy who happened to turn up where we were a couple of times. After all, it's not against the law to look.

But why did he turn up? Twice?

Chapter 36.

"This is funny," Jade whispered when we edged close to the seals at the guano-coated island. "Every time I think I'm seeing a shiny black rock, it raises a smooth head, swings its neck and slithers into the water. And all those black 'clumps of moss' swim to the island and bounce up on their flippers. There must be a thousand seals out here."

"Never in the entire harbor of Shanghai have I seen such a sight," said Lee, watching seals surround the boat.

"We'll move in close enough for you to get a look at the crabs, too. If you watch, you'll see them swarming all over the island," Eric said.

"How did you know about this island?" I asked. "I've never been here, and you know how long we've vacationed in San Carlos."

"Other divers told me about it, so when I brought my kids to San Carlos last winter, we chartered a boat out of Guaymas and cruised over here. My girls are nuts over animals and I wanted them to see how these seals, crabs and birds live in their natural habitat."

I raised my eyebrows at Jade and silently asked her about Eric. I didn't know anything about his personal life, only what I knew from seeing him in Dad's office.

"Eric has been divorced for a long time, but he sees his two little girls almost every day and they have a good relationship. I don't know what kind of relationship the children have with Sandy because I've been away at school. Dad and I hope Eric and Sandy will get married. We think they'd make a nice family."

"We'll back off from the rocks and keep more depth under us now—I'd hate to shear a propeller blade—and circle the island. We want to look for the most favorable place to drop anchor and dive," Eric said, paying no attention to my conversation with Jade.

He shifted into reverse, backed away from the rocks, and cruised slowly around the island, parallel to the shore.

"There's no sand on the whole island," Sandy observed. "It's nothing but solid volcanic rock. I don't even see a place to go ashore, the cliffs are so high. They rise straight out of the sea."

"That's right," Eric said. "The water's about a hundred feet deep, and you can see how clear it is. There are several large rocks which fractured from the cliff and fell into the sea and we want to dive near them."

"What will we see down there?" Lee asked, peering into the depths.

"Large schools of damselfish, parrotfish, goatfish, grouper—sometimes golden grouper, even. Good stands of Gorgonian corals, too."

We circled the entire island. Seagulls, boobies, frigates and terns wheeled above us. Large crabs skittered over the rocks, and seals and porpoises frolicked playfully.

"Look at that big black thing!" Jade yelled and pointed back to open sea. "It looks like a monster bat.

"That's a manta ray," I laughed. "See the scooped snoot and the white underside? Watch it fly through the air and then splash into the sea."

"Oh, there's a baby manta," Jade squealed. "Are they dangerous?"

"No, they're as gentle as pets. I've seen them play around our boat so close we could scratch their backs with an oar. And if we keep our eyes open, we might even see some grey whales today."

"Bill and Lee, will you get the anchors ready? I'll maneuver toward the quiet area between the cliff and that submerged pinnacle," Eric said. "The boat will be directly over a reef where the fish congregate."

Bill and Lee hauled an anchor to the bow. Sandy, Jade and I made sure we were clear of the coil of line. We didn't want it to wrap around our feet as it uncoiled into deep water.

Chapter 37.

"That's fine. Drop the other anchor off the stern," Eric shouted over the roar of surf smashing against the cliff.

"Shall we bring up the diving equipment?" Bill yelled.

"Yes, and one of us will need to stay in the boat while the others dive."

"I'll stay," Lee offered.

"Thanks, Lee, but why don't I stay here while the rest of you dive? When you've had enough and want to come up, you can take a break I'll dive," Eric proposed.

Sandy looked disappointed. "Sure you don't mind?"

"Not a bit. I'll put out the diving flag, help you get ready and keep an eye on you."

"Then we'll come back for you in a little while and some of us will go back down with you," Sandy promised.

We hadn't dived from a boat before, but Eric and Sandy had rehearsed us by having us dive off the dock and then swim back to it and exit the water. We knew how to do it properly, and now we found it was even easier to dive from the platform on the stern.

Dressed in our .wetsuits, masks and fins, our equipment checked and double-checked, we splashed feet first into the crystal water.

Sandy and Jade buddied, swimming deeper and deeper. Bill led Lee and me a short way behind.

So this was the undersea world! No wonder Monsieur Jacque Cousteau had made a life of it! Never had I seen so many colors, shapes and sizes of fish and brilliant coral. I spotted an octopus, but he saw me, too, and squirted a cloud of black ink and whooshed away like a stealth bomber.

I glanced at the dive computer on my wrist. We'd been in the water for nearly an hour, but it seemed like fifteen minutes.

Bill signaled that it was time to ascend, and I saw Sandy and Jade already swimming toward the surface.

"How was it?" Eric asked as he helped us climb into the boat and shuck our tanks.

"Fantastic!" Lee exclaimed. "This is the most extraordinary experience of my life!"

"Mine, too," Jade said. "Pueblo Indians in Denver don't see a lot of ocean scuba diving."

"Cherokees in Texas don't either," I added. "If they'd known about this, they'd have left the forests and plains generations ago."

"Hot chocolate?" Eric asked, the big thermos in his hand.

"Yes, kind sir." Sandy shivered and reached for a steaming mug.

We warmed up, watched the birds and seals, talked about the fish we saw and tried to identify each one.

When we were rested, Sandy asked, "Who wants to dive again?"

"I'll stay in the boat this time. Eric, you and the others go down," Bill offered.

We dressed again and dived. Diving was becoming easier each time I went into the depths. I was now so comfortable in this watery environment that I was perfectly relaxed swimming along watching the rich sea life.

Too soon, Eric signaled us to ascend.

"Wow! That was terrific," Eric exclaimed, water streaming off his wet suit as he climbed out of the sea "Let's stow our equipment and eat lunch. By then it'll be time to start back. The wind's coming up, and away from the lee of the island, the water's white-capping. It might be a rough ride home."

"That's exciting!" I said, elated. "I love storms at sea. I pretend I'm in a Joseph Conrad adventure and I'm the valiant unflinching heroine who is never shaken. I'm really good at storms. You can trust me on that."

Bill raised his eyebrows and grinned. "We'll see.

Chapter 38.

"Bill, do you mind getting life jackets for everyone? I don't like the looks of the clouds in the west, and the wind has shifted 180 degrees," Eric shouted over the roar of wind and waves.

"Glad to," Bill yelled back and climbed down the steps into the bow.

"Where are they?" he called from below after several minutes of hunting.

"In the storage chest. In that cubbyhole behind the ice box."

Another five minutes passed. The boat rocked crazily as we moved out of the lee of the island and into the full force of the wind.

"They aren't there," Bill said and came on deck. "I looked in the storage chest, under the bunks, behind the stairs and even in the head. The life jackets are not there. Any other ideas?"

Lee frowned. "I know the jackets were in the storage chest. Eric and I checked and counted them last night when we fueled the boat."

"Well, they're not there anymore," Bill stated.

"In that case, everybody will have to stay seated during the trip. We're starting to bounce around pretty badly, and there's a squall line moving toward us. We'll try to outrun it, but the sea is already too rough for much speed."

We had begun to shiver even before the clouds covered the sun, and now it was really chilly.

"Here are your windbreakers," Bill said and handed them to us. "Try to stay dry."

When we cleared the tip of the rocky island the wind hit the boat broadside and jolted it hard. Carefully watching the direction of the waves, Eric quartered the boat into them and turned toward home. Moments later, the first spatters of cold raindrops began to drill holes in the sea.

The boat growled and labored out of one deep trough only in time for a swell to roll toward us, pass underneath, lift the boat high on its crest and force us into a precipitous slide down the other side. We were on a roller coaster far scarier than any I'd ridden in amusement parks.

The pitching and plunging of the boat made me awfully queasy. It was obvious that this ocean storm was not one for anyone to trust me on, after all. I was neither valiant nor unflinching. Instead, I was industrial-strength sick.

Bill and Lee stood next to Eric, watching for rocks and crashing waves. Sandy, Jade and I hunkered down low enough that we were somewhat protected from the cold wind and piercing salt spray.

Another swell, more gigantic than the one before, rolled toward us, threatening to strike the boat broadside and capsize it. Eric wrestled with the steering and tried with all his strength to position the boat to face the swell bow-on.

Suddenly, terrifyingly, at the height of the struggle, our inboard/outboard motor died. The SATIN DOLL pitched and twisted, out of control.

We hung on to the railing, sure we'd be thrown out of the boat when the next swell hit and we'd vanish forever in this raging, frenzied sea.

Chapter 39.

Dumbfounded and desperate, Eric tried repeatedly to start the engine but it wouldn't fire. The boat was tortured by a sea beast which clenched us in its grip at the crest of gigantic waves, then tossed us into the trough like a child tired of a toy. We held on for dear life.

"Let me try it," Bill yelled into Eric's ear. "Maybe I can get it started."

No luck. The engine was dead.

Another swell rumbled toward us. We rose on its crest, then sashayed sideways. The next swell smacked us broadside. Cold, salty waves broke over the top of the boat, drenched us, flooded the seats and carpet and spilled down the steps into the bow.

"Keep trying to start it. Lee, hold the wheel. I'm going to look at the engine," Eric yelled in the gale.

"Sandy, help me raise this engine cover. And hold on," he shouted.

The boat rocked like a cradle shoved by a maniac. Eric and Sandy couldn't stand up without holding tightly to the side rails. Step by cautious step, they crept toward the stern and the housing that covered the engine.

His fingers stiff from cold, Eric unfastened the clips on the cover and he and Sandy gradually pried it open.

Sandy held on to the boat rail with one hand and tried to steady Eric with the other while he looked into the complex engine.

"I can't see anything wrong," he shouted. "There aren't any loose wires, and I don't see any prob—."

A fierce blast of wind hit us and ripped the engine cover out of Eric's hands, snapped it off the hinges and carried it sailing into the stormy sea.

"Eric, are you okay?" Sandy gasped. "Get down. You'll be thrown out of the boat!"

Jade and I, wet and worried, watched them move slowly and carefully toward Bill in the cockpit. Icy water was running down his head and neck but he was just standing there. Not steering, not trying to start the motor, just staring at the dash panel.

"Bill, can't you get it started?" Eric asked. "I didn't see any problem with the motor."

Bill's eyes narrowed. He glared at Eric. Lee, shoulders slumped and defeated, looked hopelessly out to sea.

"I know what the problem is," Bill said bitterly, clenching his fists.

"Well, what?" Eric demanded impatiently.

"No gas."

"No gas? Impossible! Lee and I filled the tank to the brim last night. There's enough gas in that tank to take us from the marina to this island and back, with plenty left over. We have more than enough gas."

"See for yourself." Bill stepped away from the cockpit and turned the controls over to Eric. Eric's eyes locked onto the gauges on the panel.

"It *is* empty! Damn it! How could that happen?"

The men stood at the windshield watching the sky growing darker, the rain squall moving toward us, horrendous swells piling up and rolling forward.

"What can we do?" I asked.

"I'll get the flares. We're near a favorite reef for fishermen, and the commercial shrimp boats ply the sea lane north of the island on their way to Guaymas and the shrimp processing plants," Eric said and hurried below.

When he returned, he was empty-handed. "Did somebody move the flares?"

We shook our heads.

"I'll look," Sandy offered and crawled across the soggy carpet.

She climbed into the bucking bow, holding tightly to the door frame. In a few minutes, she emerged. "The flares are gone."

"Then we're in real trouble," Bill said. "No gas. No flares. No life jackets. No radio or depth finder."

"Sandy, Jade, Velvet, I need you to go below. Wrap up in the sleeping bags on the bunks and stay there. I don't want you to get bashed up in all this rolling and lurching," Eric ordered.

"Lee, tie yourself to the rail and keep a look-out for boats on the horizon behind us. Bill, you and I'll watch ahead and to port and starboard. We do have this red towel. If anybody sees a fishing boat or a shrimper, wave it for all you're worth. The storm will have to blow over, someone will have to find us, or this is a done deal. A bad done deal."

Chapter 40.

We huddled, wet and shivering, inside the bow. The bunk mattresses were damp, the sleeping bags soggy and cold. One moment we were thrown forward and the next tossed back. The scuba tanks rolled and clanked against each other in spite of padding we'd packed around them when we wedged them into the storage area as best we could.

No bronc buster on my father's Texas ranch ever had a wilder, scarier ride than we had as the boat plunged, pitched and rocked.

"Just hold on," Sandy soothed. "It's better that we bounce around on these bunks than crash on the floor."

"What's going to happen?" Jade asked, frightened. I was plenty scared myself.

"I don't know," I admitted. "I think this storm is what the Mexicans call a chubasco. I've heard about them but I've never seen one before. They arrive in summertime with raging winds and crashing waves. Tropical storms can move in unexpectedly and fast, and can blow over just as quickly. Or, they can race all the way from the Pacific Ocean, cross the Baja Peninsula, and gain strength over the warm waters of the Sea of Cortez. I just don't know what this one is going to do."

We looked up and saw Bill cautiously climbing down the steps into the bow. He looked at us huddling together and laughed. "This isn't funny, but I'd sure like a picture of you like this to show you after we get back to the States. Instead of THREE BLIND MICE, you're THREE DROWNED MICE."

"You're a rather wet blanket, yourself, counselor. Those chill bumps and red ears don't do much for you, either," Sandy teased. "What's the storm like now?"

"Truth? It's worse. There's no break in the clouds in any direction. The wind is almost gale force and the rain is pouring down. If we don't crash on that rocky island and founder, it'll be only by the grace of God. "

"Is there anything we can do? For you?" I asked.

"Yes, there is. I think we'd better send one person at a time down here to warm up while the other two watch for boats, and we'll rotate. I want to send Lee first."

"That's fine; we'll do the best we can to get him warm. Take care of yourselves, too," Sandy said.

Moments later, Lee struggled through the storm to reach the steps and climb into the bow. "Lee, come huddle with us," Jade said. "Hold on, though. We don't want you to bash your head on the ice box."

Soaked to the skin and shaking uncontrollably from the cold, Lee snuggled into the space Jade and I made between us.

"Thanks," he said with chattering teeth. "You offered me a vacation I'd never forget, and I'm sure I never will."

There wasn't much heat in the wet sleeping bags, but the warmth from our bodies was enough that Lee finally stopped shaking. It helped just to be out of the wind and cold spray, I was sure.

We hushed, listening to the roar of the storm, trying to keep from rolling off the bunk and praying we would survive until the winds and waves abated.

Jade looked down at Lee and smiled. Curious as to what was amusing, Sandy and I looked at him, too. Lee, packed in the bunk with us like one more chilled sardine, was sound asleep, oblivious to the raging storm and grim predicament we were in.

Chapter 41.

"A boat! A shrimp boat! We need you on deck," Eric yelled into our marine cave.

Lee awakened with a jerk, momentarily confused as to where he was. We threw off the sleeping bags and scrambled up on deck.

"On the left, coming up behind us. Whatever you have, jackets, towels, anything, wave them," Eric ordered.

The swells were still as high as ever and the troughs were as deep. Cold rain pelted us, but low on the horizon, a narrow band of blue sky promised an end to the storm, and a shrimp boat off our stern gave us hope we would be rescued.

It wasn't time to rejoice yet, though; we'd drifted dangerously close to the black cliffs of the rocky island. I had no doubt the boat would smash on them and shatter into splinters if we weren't rescued soon.

"Keep waving," Bill yelled.

We watched the heavy, sluggish shrimp boat crawl through the high seas. *Dear God, let them see us*, I prayed. *Make them look this way.*

Anxiously, we strained to see through the torrent of rain. Then, miraculously, it stopped. An opening broke in the black clouds and brilliant sunshine poured through the hole like a spotlight on a stage, and our white boat was right in the center of it.

We waved our jackets and towels as though we were the only survivors on a desert island seeing the one ship of the year.

HONK. HONK. HONK, signaled the shrimp boat.

"I think they see us," I yelled.

And they did. The big shrimper with its arms folded and looking like an arthritic grasshopper gradually reduced speed and turned toward us.

"I don't think we can stay off the rocks much longer," Eric worried aloud as he estimated our meager distance from the island. "And, if we get too near the island, the shrimper won't be able to get close enough to tie on."

Time stopped. We forgot the wind and waves. Forgot the pitching and yawing of the boat. All we did was hang on until the lumbering shrimper reached us.

"Thank God," Jade murmured. "I thought we were going to die, and drowning would be a terrible way to go. I think almost any way would be better than that.""You won't have to worry any more, Jade," Eric said. "Everything is going to be all right. You can count on living to a ripe old age and telling your grandchildren about the day you went to San Pedro Island to scuba dive."

That was reassuring. I had about given up the idea of old age or grandchildren. Or diving, dancing, finishing college, or marrying Bill. Now I could put my dreams back together. Especially of marrying Bill.

Chapter 42.

As soon as a stocky, grizzly seaman on the shrimp boat threw a cable to us, Bill tied it securely and signaled we were ready to be towed out of this storm.

The captain waved and ordered his crew to begin towing. Heavy motors revved and the propeller churned a path of foam which we followed toward bays that were relatively sheltered from the wind.

Our wild sea became mercifully calm; sun broke through the clouds, the rain stopped, and the wind died

"I think the shrimper is too big to enter San Carlos Bay," Eric said when we rounded the last point of land. "My guess is the captain will radio for a towboat from our marina to meet us, turn us over to it, and then resume his trip into Guaymas."

Sure enough, at the mouth of San Carlos Bay, a dilapidated towboat waited for us, rocking gently on the peaceful water.

"That's Roberto!" I exclaimed. "He didn't send anyone; he came himself."

The captain of the shrimp boat supervised as his boat reduced speed and let the towline go slack. Bill untied the line and dropped it into the water. Crewmen pulled it aboard the shrimper, waved, and shouted good luck to us. The captain turned his attention to his job, increased the ship's speed, and plowed toward the sea lane to Guaymas.

Roberto maneuvered his towboat close to us. We tied the towline and were slowly pulled toward the marina. Now that we were safe, I thought about the storm that struck us and caused us such concern, and I made a considered decision. Some women don't do floors; some don't do windows. From now on, I don't do tropical storms.

Almost too tired to move, I followed our group out of the boat onto the dock.

"What happened?" Roberto asked. "Motor trouble?"

Bill and Eric looked grim.

"No. Not motor trouble. Out of fuel," Eric said.

"Where did you go? You took on enough fuel last night to run up the coast all the way to Puerto Penasco. You didn't go that far, did you?"

"No. We only went to San Pedro Island. We ran out of gas there," Bill said.

"There's something screwy about it, too," Eric said. "We filled the tank late last night—you saw us—and stowed the life jackets and flares. We made sure the boat was ready for this trip. But when we tried to leave the island and come home this afternoon, we didn't have any fuel or life jackets or flares."

Roberto scowled.

"Was there anybody messing with the boat during the night?" Eric asked.

"I don't see how," Roberto said, pausing, thinking. "We locked up and went home right after you left, and the night watchman patrolled the docks all night. Do you want to talk to him?"

"I think we'd better," Bill said.

"Jade, you're the most fluent in Spanish. Will you interpret for us?" Eric asked.

"Sure. I was helpless to converse in China and Lee had to interpret everyplace we went. I'd love to practice a language I know."

We walked up the dock to the marina office. A neatly-uniformed man stood at the counter reading the roster of boats moored in the harbor.

"Tomás Santiago," Roberto indicated. "My watchman for twenty years."

The watchman extended his hand to the men, and Bill introduced Sandy and Jade. I already knew him; Dad had introduced him last winter when we were here.

"Pleased to meet you," he said in Spanish. "Miss Shepard, nice to see you again. Is the senator here?"

My mastery of Spanish didn't extend beyond ordinary conversation needed in stores and service stations and marinas, not enough to carry on a conference, so I said no, sorry, my father wasn't here, and hushed.

"Tomás, these folks fueled the SATIN DOLL late last evening, checked it for a diving trip, and stored their life jackets and flares. Out at San Pedro Island they ran out of fuel, and their jackets and flares were missing. Did you see anybody monkeying around the boat after I left last night?" Roberto asked in Spanish.

"No, sir. No one was here any time," Tomás answered, shaking his head.

"Ask him if he heard anything," Eric said to Jade.

She translated the question into Spanish.

Tomás again shook his head, then hesitated. "Well, maybe I did. A little while after everybody left, I thought I heard footsteps on the dock, but they were muffled. Maybe like sponge soles. Or sandals wrapped in rags. I walked down all the docks and investigated, but I didn't see anybody."

Roberto's lips pursed; his brow furrowed in thought. "I walked toward the parking area and heard a car door squeak and then tires rolling through the dirt. No lights, no motor, no door slamming. I thought it was a little strange, and I kept a sharp eye out all night, but nothing happened," Tomás said.

Roberto began to pace the office while Jade interpreted the statement to us.

"I'm going to call the police," Roberto pronounced and picked up the phone. "I think someone was deliberately malicious. Somebody wanted to harm you. What did you do to make an enemy way down here?"

Chapter 43.

"Use my office," Roberto said after he introduced Chief of Police Salinas and Captain Morales. "I'm going to close the door if you don't mind. No sense alarming everybody."

Roberto waved the chief into a cracked, peeling leather, swivel chair behind the desk. The rest of us sat on metal folding chairs rusty around the bolts with vinyl seats grimy from years of use in a boat yard.

"Roberto said you had some trouble at San Pedro Island. Want to tell me about it?" Chief Salinas asked.

Eric began, "Last night, late, about ten, ten thirty, we came by boat from the Playa de Cortez. Lee and I stayed here to fuel the boat and check it for a diving expedition while Bill took the women home. Lee and I counted the life jackets and flares and stored them in the chest in the bow. When we finished, we walked up to the parking lot and a few minutes later Bill drove over and picked us up."

The officers listened alertly while Eric told about what happened during the storm at the island.

"Were there been any other suspicious events before that?" the chief asked.

"Not really suspicious, but there have been several things that made us a little nervous. Velvet, why don't you tell them about your horseback ride?" Bill urged.

I told them about seeing the body the police were digging up near the airstrip; the cave full of weapons, clothes and canned food; our horses driven from where we tied them to the palms; and the rabbit with its throat slashed and its eyes punched out.

Jade said, "And remember the tan car and driver that seemed to be checking us out when we were in your carport? Also, I don't know whether it means anything or not, but when I was water skiing at Algodones, there was a man in a rental boat sitting and watching me. When I skied past him, he made a slashing gesture across his throat."

"What did he look like?" the chief asked.

"It's hard to say. I was skiing fast and trying so hard to stay on my feet I didn't pay that much attention. He wasn't really close enough for me to see him clearly, anyway."

"Mexican? American? Old? Young? Size?" the chief pressed.

"Not Mexican. His skin was dark but it was from the sun. He didn't have a shirt on. Young, I think. Muscular. Maybe like a surfer."

"It wasn't Pablo?" I asked Jade, still suspicious of our gardener. "Oh, no. He didn't look anything like Pablo. Probably more like the guy you described who was in the shadows of the hotel last night, the one who left before anyone got a good look at him," Jade said.

"Anything else?" the chief asked.

"Do you know a Mexican named Pablo?" I asked. "Short, stocky, walks with a limp? Wears huaraches with rubber-tire soles?"

"Yes. Pablo Ortiz. Everybody knows him. He's a good man. Just a little different from other people. You don't have to worry about him. Why?"

"He's taking care of our yard this summer, and we didn't know him before," I answered. "He just appeared out of the blue and I thought he acted threatening."

"Pablo is perfectly safe. There's no reason at all for concern. Now, if there's nothing more you can tell us about the other man and events, would you show us your boat? Before we leave this office, though, I do want to say I agree with Roberto that someone was deliberately malicious. Why, I don't know. We've had two murders recently, but I don't see anything that would tie either one of them to the problems you've had. We'll have to look deeper into this thing before we can figure it out."

Bill looked thoughtful, uneasy.

The chief continued. "If I were you, I'd stick together and stay close to shore. Lock your house at night and when you leave. Keep your eyes open for anybody or anything that seems suspicious. If you see something, give us a call. Most of your neighbors are in the States for the summer, and they don't have phones in their houses, anyway, but there are phones here at the marina, and also at the cantina and at Posada de San Carlos. Either Captain Morales or I will look into anything you report."

We listened, apprehensive.

The chief stood, then as an afterthought, said, "Most of all, you need to know that both of the murders were of American young women, small, with black hair. A lot like both of you." He looked pointedly at Jade and me.

Attempting to digest the not-so-veiled warning, we filed out of the office, across the parking lot and down the dock to the

SATIN DOLL. The officers stepped aboard, examined the layout, the drenched sleeping bags and bunks, the EMPTY reading on the gas gauge, and the bare engine with no cover.

Apparently satisfied, Chief Salinas said, "We'll talk with some folks and ask a few questions, climb up to the cave and look around, find out what we can. It may take us a while to get to the bottom of this. In the meantime, if you do any more diving, do it close to shore. We'll be in touch as soon as we have anything to tell you. Until later, good afternoon."

Chapter 44.

"Aren't you the sleepy-heads today?" Maria teased as we straggled one by one to the kitchen. "You're usually up and on the beach before the sun. Did you play too hard yesterday?"

"Um-hum. Something like that," I mumbled, tiredly.

"I think you better go back to bed. You look like a sick seagull after a typhoon."

"That's close enough," I agreed.

"Does anybody want to do anything special today?" Eric asked.

"Yes. Sleep."

"Lay out."

"Paint."

"I have an idea," I said. "We could drive into Guaymas later in the day and bum around. I haven't shown you the outdoor markets or shrimp-processing plants, and there's a terrific seafood restaurant on the bay. We could even drive down the coast to Empalme and Playa del Sol."

"What are they?" Sandy asked.

"Empalme is a town south of Guaymas, and Playa del Sol is a gorgeous beach west of there. You ought to paint it," I answered, enthusiastic about my idea even if it was like bragging about my own cooking. "I haven't had a chance to treat anyone yet. Why don't you let me take you to the seafood restaurant for lunch? After we eat we can go sightseeing."

"We'd love it," Sandy beamed. "I'll take a sketch pad and camera. I've heard about Mexican outdoor markets but I've never seen one."

"It's quite a sight," Eric said, "lots of color and noise. Counters of fresh fish and shrimp, racks of beef and chickens, pyramids of tropical fruit and vegetables, handmade pottery, and serapes and rugs."

"That sounds a lot like the markets in China," Lee said, surprised. "I'll take my camera, too, and send photos home to my family."

"Will we have to dress up?" Jade asked.

"No. Jeans and sandals are all right. Some Americans wear shorts, but they attract a lot of attention."

Bill smiled. "You women are enough to attract attention in a gunny sack, never mind shorts. We'll probably need armed guards to get you out of town."

"Oh, Bill," I said, "that's all hype. Nobody's even going to look twice. You're just stroking our egos. But don't stop."

Penny laughed. "Then we're agreed? We'll go?"

"We're agreed," the others answered.

"Is 11:30 okay?" I asked.

"Perfect," Bill said. "We'll be together, away from here, and forget about everything else. It'll be a nice, relaxed day compared with yesterday."

"Anything will be more relaxed than yesterday," Sandy said. "I have so many tension kinks they might never unravel. I need some time at my easel before I'm normal again."

Chapter 45.

The men went to the storage room and took care of our diving equipment while we showered and shampooed. By the time we were dressed and ready to go to Guaymas, the men were also clean and dressed.

"Eric, will you drive? You know your way around town," I suggested.

"Sure. The Pescado Restaurant first?"

"Yes, let's."

The Pescado, on the other side of the bay from downtown Guaymas, was shaded by fire trees and bougainvilleas. The cool, dark interior was decorated with fish nets and brightly-colored glass floats. Picture windows overlooked white sailboats bobbing in the blue harbor. I could tell Sandy was painting in her mind.

I tried hard to keep from thinking about all the strange things that had happened lately, but I couldn't keep from looking into shadows and wondering if someone was watching.

I think everyone else felt the same way. We tried to keep the mood light and talked about the outdoor market, and then the menu. Nothing bad could happen with good food. We decided to order fresh steamed clams and mussels, fried oysters, and red snapper with a spicy sauce of tomatoes, onions and peppers, and everybody shared family style.

Our waiter kept the bread basket filled with crusty hot bolillos, and at the end of lunch he brought a tray of sliced pineapple, bananas, papayas, mangoes and guavas for dessert.

"Enough," Sandy declared. "Any more good food and I'll look like Santa Claus."

Eric ignored her excellent figure and said, "You're absolutely right. Just look at that paunch!" He signaled our waiter and said, "Quick! Our check! The lady needs her sleigh. She's needed at the North Pole at once."

"She what? Oh. Right. One minute, sir." He hurried to the kitchen and moments later we heard a blast of laughter from the manager and cook. "Oh, Chihuahua! Thees Americanos they do like the joke. Tell them we don't have no sleigh, but the harbor ees full of boats. Tell them Mexico ees much nicer than the North Pole."

We went outside to our scorching car, locked and hot enough to sizzle an egg. And our brains. Even the velour upholstery smelled baked. We'd have welcomed a trip to the North Pole.

"To the market?" Eric asked.

"To the market," we chorused.

Sandy and Lee, fascinated by the riotous colors of produce and native-made goods, clicked their cameras and took picture after picture while Jade and Bill watched and listened to the babble of Spanish and Indian, cries of babies, bleating of goats, and the clucking of poultry in wooden pens.

"It's an overload to the senses," Sandy said, amazed.

"Have you seen enough?" Eric asked when we began to wilt from the stifling heat.

"For now. But I have to paint these scenes before we leave Mexico," Sandy said. "When can we come back?"

Eric said, "How about tomorrow, if we don't dive? I'll come with you."

We returned to our oven-on-wheels and drove through Guaymas. I pointed out the sights: the dock with charter boats for sport fishing, shrimp boats tied to the pier, unloading their catch for the processing plants, and foreign oil tankers anchored in the harbor.

Outside town we wound south on a two-lane blacktop parallel to the railroad, past refineries that belched smelly, black smoke into the turquoise sky, and over salt flats fed by a lagoon.

"Lots of trucks and trains," Bill observed.

"Yes, they're major forms of transportation here. And, you'll also see plenty of buses, donkey carts, men riding bicycles to work, and people on foot," I said, enjoying being the tour guide again.

"Where's that beach you told us about, the Playa del Sol?" Eric asked.

"The next town is Empalme. Stay on the main road all the way through town, and a little way south there's a turn-off to the west. We'll take a dirt road across the desert and dunes to the beach."

"Is that it?" Eric asked a few miles later.

He slowed down. The weathered wooden sign at the turn-off lay broken on the sand but I recognized the place.

"Yes. Turn right. This road doesn't look like much, but it's the only one to the Playa."

I hadn't been able to get rid of the fear that we were being watched, and I'd been glancing behind us, looking for an old tan Ford. But if anyone was following us, he could have stayed out of sight behind any of the buses and trucks. Now, on a dirt road, any vehicle would stir up a lot of dust and we'd know it was there.

I relaxed.

Our car wallowed in sand deep enough to trap us and raised a cloud of dust that hovered in the still air, then settled in thick layers on the windshield and hood. Waves of heat rose from the sizzling sand. Cactus, ocotillo and dry, brown grass were the only signs of life in the harsh desert.

"Straight ahead between those two big sand dunes," I directed. The car labored through deep ruts between them and in a single instant the landscape of dreary, arid wasteland opened to a panorama of peaceful aqua sea.

"It's glorious!" Sandy exclaimed, and was first to step out of the car onto the broad beach.

Jade kicked off her sandals and ran to the water, letting the gentle surf cool her toes.

"The water's shallow a long way from shore, isn't it?" Bill asked. "You could walk a hundred yards and not even be waist deep."

"That's right. This is where Dad comes surf fishing. He likes to wade out to where you see those rollers and stand there, shoulder deep, hour after hour, casting for corvinas. He says it relaxes him. Do you like to fish? We have surf rods in the storage room. Would you like to use them?" I asked.

"Yes! How about fishing with me?"

"I'd rather go beachcombing, if you don't mind. Why don't we ask the rest of the gang to come with us and make a day of it? This is probably the safest beach on the entire coast. Hardly anybody knows how to get here. We can fish and swim and have a picnic, and not worry about maliciousness," I said with certainty.

"What time do you have, Eric?" Sandy asked during the drive home.

"Five-fifteen. Why? Is there something else you want to do?"

"I was just thinking, we'll only be in San Carlos a few more days. It's too late to go today, but I'd like to make another open water dive."

"And I still want to take you to the estuary to dig clams and catch crabs," I reminded them.

Eric said, "Why don't we plan to dive at Haystack Rock early tomorrow? It's close to shore, and our diving guidebook says it's one of the best locations in the area."

"Yes, let's do that, and when the tide's low we can run to the estuary by boat. We can drop anchor at the mouth of the lagoon and swim across to the clam beds. While we're there, I can show you the mangrove jungle and egrets," I suggested. "Do you know how to cook clams and crabs?" Jade asked.

"Oh, sure. We can bring them home and have a clambake in our own cove at the base of the cliff."

"Are we all agreed?" Sandy asked.

"Yes, that'll be fun."

Eric said, "This time we'll wait 'til morning to fuel the boat and load it."

"I'll be responsible for the life jackets and flares," Lee declared. "If I'm on that boat, you can be absolutely certain our equipment is, too."

Chapter 46.

We arose at sunup, ate breakfast and loaded our scuba gear into the van.

"We'll need windbreakers for a while," Eric said, "and you might even want to put on your wetsuits and wear them in the boat. The air will be chilly."

"Velvet, would you like to trade wetsuits today? You wear my passionate pink suit and mask, and I'll wear your fluorescent blue?" Jade asked. We'd traded clothes all week, and had agreed to trade wetsuits, too.

"Sure, but that pink is so bright I'll practically glow in the dark."

"Yes, but I doubt if you'll scare any fish with it, and I'm certain nobody will lose sight of you. Anybody will be able to spot you a mile away."

We watched Lee conscientiously count the new life jackets we bought at the marina dive shop, and place them with a bundle of flares where they'd be easily accessible and dry. Bill and Eric fueled the boat and stowed our air tanks and other gear. Sandy, Jade and I arranged the bunk mattresses, sleeping bags and dry clothing.

"Is that the hot chocolate?" Sandy asked when I handed the thermos to her. "Let's slip it into this niche."

"Okay, men, you get the rest of the day off," I said. "This is our treat today. We're going to crew the boat and let you sightsee."

I climbed onto the captain's chair and Jade cast off. I piloted the boat away from the dock and into the marina while Sandy watched the traffic.

"All clear. The channel's yours," she said.

From the time I was a little kid I've loved to be on the ocean, wind blowing my hair, salt spray on my face and sunshine on my back. Now, grown up and surrounded by friends, I'd never been happier.

"Is that where we're going? Is that Haystack Rock?" Sandy asked, pointing ahead. "It looks like a solid white mountain in the sea."

"It is solid rock, but the white is bird guano. The natives harvest it," I said.

"The guidebook says the water's eighty feet deep on the south side," Bill commented.

"That's right. It's clear, too. See those huge rocks below us? The current here is unusually strong, so we'll have to circle the island until we find a diving site that's in the lee," Eric said.

"That spot looks sheltered," Bill pointed. "Out from that pinnacle. Let's drop anchor there."

"You wouldn't be backseat driving, would you, Bill? Do I detect a tiny bit of distrust of the captain's judgement?" I asked, half joking but half serious, too.

I cut the motor and Jade the dropped anchor. We systematically unpacked the scuba gear and helped each other shrug into it and fasten the clasps.

"Velvet, would you buddy with me?" Bill asked.

"Oh, yes! I've been dying to since the very first day!" I exclaimed in my usual style. Subtle and coy.

Lee said, "I want to stay in the boat while the rest of you dive. I've never had a chance to watch porpoises and mantas play, and now's the time. If any of you want to make a second dive later, I'll go with you, but for now, do you mind if I stay on top?"

"We don't mind at all," Bill said. "Enjoy yourself, and we'll come up in a little while so you can have a chance to dive. There's plenty to see above water, but it's even more exciting below. This is something you won't want to miss!"

Chapter 47.

Sandy splashed into the sea feet first, then Jade. Eric followed. I waited a few moments and allowed them some space before I jumped in. Underwater, I glanced over my shoulder and saw Bill behind me and slightly above, swimming relaxed and easy, watching the sea life.

I swam toward the floor of the ocean. Bright orange, lacy coral sea fans grew from undersea boulders I kicked slowly and carefully, partly to linger and admire them, partly to keep from brushing them with my fins or tank and damaging the fragile tips.

Enchanted, I drifted slowly with the current and came across a school of brilliant blue and gold angel-fish, and other exotic tropicals I'd never seen.

Bill pointed to a large grouper, its drab brownish-green blotches camouflaging it against the background of a rocky cave. I swam closer to examine the homely fish, but a flash of gold swam below me from the other direction and I forgot everything else. I kicked with my fins and followed the dazzling fish toward the big grouper's cave.

The golden fish was joined by a second one. Maybe they were the exotic golden groupers my father and other fishermen often talked about but seldom saw.

At first, the fish didn't seem to care that I was following them and they swam on toward the cave, unafraid. At the entrance to the cave, however, Mr. Grouper and Friend decided I was a passionate pink alien from another world and whooshed quickly inside.

I stopped, disappointed to lose them, but a diver doesn't explore dark, underwater caves alone. Divers don't abandon their buddies, either, not even for two minutes like I'd just done. Some buddy I turned out to be! I turned to go look for Bill.

Right away I glimpsed the dark form of a diver above me. Good! Bill had found me and I wouldn't have to go back and look. Maybe we could enter the cave together.

But then the diver, pale hair streaming in the current, dived directly at me. Not toward me, but at me. He was deliberately going to collide with me! I wanted to yell, "Bill, what do you think you're doing?"

Momentarily I was paralyzed with anger, and in that single moment a gloved hand reached out, ripped the regulator out of my mouth and tore the mask off my face. He turned and darted out of sight, dragging my regulator and mask in his fist.

My God! What was happening? That wasn't Bill! Who was it? Why did he steal my regulator? What was I going to do? I was in seventy feet of water with no air supply!

Scared, I kicked and swam toward the surface, burning up what little air was in my lungs much faster than I could afford. I was rapidly running out of air. That was bad enough, but also my contact lenses had floated away when my mask was ripped off, and what had been an exquisite watery paradise was now a cloudy blur.

I knew I wouldn't be able to hold my breath long enough to reach the surface; my lungs were already nearly empty. Soon I'd gasp and open my mouth even if I didn't mean to and my lungs would fill with sea water. I was going to drown!

Then, to my horror, the phantom diver returned and swam directly toward me at great speed. Why? Hadn't he already guaranteed I'd drown? What more could he do to me?

I spent my last ounce of strength flailing my arms and legs in a desperate attempt to rise to safety but the diver grabbed me from behind, clamped his hands on my shoulders and jerked me around to face him. I was terrified, my eyes only inches from his. He forced me to look into his face. The eyes behind the mask, eyes determined and grim, were Bill's.

Holding me securely, he quickly removed his mouthpiece and placed it in my own. Air filled my scalding lungs and I gulped it thankfully. One moment earlier, I thought I'd drown. Now I knew I was saved.

Bill calmed me enough to follow the instructions for buddy breathing and I carefully returned the regulator to him the way I was supposed to. He swam strongly and steadily, continued to share his air supply, and led me to the surface and a world of air. He and Lee lifted me into the boat, wrapped me in a sleeping bag and lay me on a lounge.

I was still shivering from cold and fear when Eric, Sandy and Jade climbed into the boat, ecstatic about their successful, exciting dive.

Then, suddenly aware something was wrong, they stopped talking in mid-sentence and stared at me, their eyes wide, the air electric.

"What happened?" Sandy demanded.

Bill, enraged, said, "There's some kind of maniac on the loose. A diver attacked Velvet at seventy feet and tried to murder her. Start the motor. We're going to the police!"

Chapter 48.

Chief Salinas questioned me across the table in our kitchen. Eric, Sandy, Lee and Jade listened, speechless. Bill stood with his arms crossed, leaning against the door, clearly worried. Maria, declaring she was one of the family with every right to be there, was belligerent. How dare anyone attack me?

"Did you get a good look at his face?" the chief asked.

"No. He was wearing a face mask, so I only saw his eyes and that was just for a moment."

"Color of hair? Long? Short?"

"Light. Straight. Mid-length. It flowed behind him in the current."

"What size was he?"

I looked around, comparing sizes. "As tall as Bill, but heavier. Not as big as Eric, though."

"Would you recognize him if you saw him again?"

"No. He moved too fast, and with a face mask and wetsuit, I wouldn't know him if he walked up and shook my hand." That was a chilling thought.

The chief turned to Lee.

"You were in the boat? What did you see?"

Lee, filled with remorse, said, "I'm afraid I didn't see anything. After everyone entered the water I watched them until they were too deep. After that, all I saw were the porpoises and mantas, a couple of feeding frenzies, and the seagulls and pelicans on Haystack Rock."

"Did you see or hear any boats?"

"None. Not around the island. Not out to sea."

"Did you see any person with or without a wet suit in the water or on the island at any time?"

Lee was miserable. He wasn't ever going to forget this vacation. What a crumby way to entertain a foreign visitor!

"No, I'm sorry, I didn't see anyone. There was no one around until Velvet and Bill came to the surface and swam to the boat." The chief surveyed each one of us seriously, probingly. Were we telling the truth? Did anyone have anything to hide? We waited in silence, each with our own thoughts and anxiety.

Bill stepped forward, leaned over the table, his arms supporting him as he spoke to the chief. "Should we leave San Carlos and go back to the States?"

The chief thought about it, straightened his back, flexed his shoulder muscles, rubbed his neck. He was as tense as the rest of us.

"No. I don't think so. You're leaving in a few days, anyway, aren't you? Why don't you stay and try to enjoy the last of your vacation, but don't anybody go off alone. Stay in twos or more. Remain on land. Don't use your boat and don't dive. We've got a couple of leads we're following up on, and if they pan out, we'll want you here to press charges. We're sorry this happened to you, and we're doing all we can to get to the bottom of it."

He scraped his chair back from the table, stood, and picked up his cap.

Bill shook his hand. "Thanks, Chief. We appreciate your help."

"You're welcome. You'll hear from us again," he said and left the house.

Silently, Maria set a pitcher of fresh limeade on the table and brought out my mother's blue glasses. That was as comforting as a baby blanket to me.

"Well?" Bill asked.

"It looks to me like someone wanted to scare Velvet away from here for some reason, and when she didn't scare, he decided to kill her," Eric said.

"What should we do?" Sandy asked.

"We should do exactly what the chief says: don't go off alone and don't use the boat until he finds the answer," Eric said. "And Velvet, will you please not go swimming or running on the beach or anyplace else without Bill or Lee or me? And no more hair-brained chasing after golden groupers!"

"Don't be too tough on her. It was as much my fault as hers. I was looking at sea corals and tropical fish when I should have been watching her and didn't see her turn," Bill said.

"I promise," I said. "I won't deny I'm scared and I'll do what the chief says. I'm truly sorry for everything. But it makes me as frustrated as a centipede on Velcro to know your vacation is almost over and you won't have a chance to do everything you came here to do."

"Better that we miss part of our vacation than for you to miss all the rest of your life," Sandy said. "I imagine we'll survive. And just to try to make it more likely, who can you think of who would have a reason to harm you? Have you made anyone angry? Or caused them a hardship? Either in Mexico or the United States."

My nerves shot, and fighting tears, I said, "If I've caused somebody a problem, I don't know who it was. I can't think of a single enemy. It doesn't make any sense at all for someone to try to kill me. I don't understand it! Some important part of this puzzle is missing, and I can't figure out what it is. Can you?"

Chapter 49.

In the afternoon Sandy set up her easel on the terrace and painted the dramatic view of Bahia de San Carlos and the Tetas de Cabras. The men fished off the peninsula for a while, then walked down the hill to the marina and washed the boat. Jade and I sunbathed in our cove at the foot of the cliff and talked about college and clothes and men—anything other than danger and death.

But I was restless. I wasn't used to lying around making small talk, especially when the real thing on my mind was so serious and sobering.

Besides, it was a waste to have places to see and things to do and not be able to do them. Especially since it was because of me. I had tried and tried to figure it out, but for the life of me, I couldn't find any reason why I would be anyone's target.

I climbed the steps up the cliff and went to the kitchen to get limeade for Jade. Maria cornered me. "Did you telephone your father? Does he know about these terrible things that have been happening?"

"No, I don't want to worry him. They'll turn out to be just a bizarre series of incidents that are all a crazy mistake and there's nothing Dad can do from Washington. Probably nothing even if he flew down here. I bet Chief Salinas will have it solved by tomorrow, and we have to leave next week, regardless."

"For now, is there something I can do for you?"

"Nothing, dear Maria. Except, you might keep your eyes open for any guy who might be the one Jade saw in the rental boat and the one I saw a couple of times and try to get a better description. A license number, too, if he drives that tan Ford. I don't suppose he'll come around here again, but he might happen to go to the market when you're there. He must have to buy groceries some time."

That evening Maria cooked one of her exotic Mexican dinners. She insisted we stay out on the terrace so we could watch the sunset with its outrageously brilliant reds and purples on the mountains and bays, but the fragrance drifting from the kitchen was so tempting we could hardly wait to eat.

"Shall we storm the kitchen and raid the pots?" Bill asked.

"No, Maria does this on purpose, tempts us with fragrances until we can't stand it another minute, then brings steaming food by the platterful. You'll see," I promised. The kitchen door opened and Maria, her eyes shining mischievously, brought a loaded tray.

Our eyes popped and our mouths watered at the sight of creamy crab enchiladas, brown beans, golden cheese, red and green salsa and golden sopaipillas. Maria saw Sandy's appraisal of the colorful arrangement and teased, "Are you going to paint this, too?""Yes, I am. Seriously. I'll take a photo of your feast and paint from that. This food isn't going to last long enough for anything else."

Appreciating the compliment, Maria said, "Enjoy your dinner. There is much more when you are ready."

"Where are we going to find food like this in Denver?" Sandy asked.

"Or Palo Alto?"

"Or Shanghai?"

"You could come back to Mexico and Maria," I said. "How does Christmas on the beach sound? Christmas with super scuba diving and no scares?"

"Great idea!" Eric exclaimed.

"Let's do it," Bill added.

While we ate we planned the holiday and deliberately avoided talking about the frightening events of this trip. Our nerves needed a night off.

"Velvet," Bill said after dinner, "about your dad's surf rods, how would you like to go back to Empalme with me tomorrow? You said hardly anyone goes there so maybe we can do some fishing and not worry about intruders."

"I'd like that. What about the rest of you guys going with us for the day?"

Sandy declined. "I'd really like to paint those market scenes. Eric, will you go with me?"

"Yes, any time."

"Jade? Lee?" I asked.

Lee said, "Thanks, but Jade and I've been wanting to run up the coast to the estuary and collect those big white sand dollars and sea shells you told us about. Do you mind?"

"Do I mind? Heavens no!" I just wished I could be a hermit crab hiding in a nearby seashell while they were there.

"Well then, Bill, let's you and I go," I said.

"Do you have a tide table?" he asked.

"Right here." I went to the desk in the living room, returned to the terrace, and handed the table to him. "The tide will be highest at eight tomorrow night."

"What do you say we leave here at four o'clock? That'll give us plenty of time to drive to the Playa and set up our rods before the best time to fish."

"Sounds good to me," I agreed. "Just as long as everyone else gets to do what they want and everybody is safe."

"We're doing exactly what we want. You don't need to entertain us. And we'll be perfectly safe, so stop worrying. Go have a good time and bring back enough fish for a meal. I want to watch what magic Maria casts over fish dinners," Sandy said. "She's going to turn me into a cook yet. But not all the time," she added, seeing Eric's hopeful grin.

Chapter 50.

"So this is where the senator catches the fish he's always telling us about," Bill said, looking at the gentle swells and shallow beach.

"This is it. Just walk up the shore about a hundred yards and wade in," I pointed. "Nobody ever comes here. There's only one road in, and there aren't any facilities for boats or people, so the fish are all yours."

"Shall I set up a rod for you?"

I shook my head. "Maybe later. I'd like to run in the surf and get rid of some of this tension, and then I want to look for sea shells while it's still light. You go ahead and fish."

"Where are you going to run? How long?"

I kissed him lightly on the cheek. "Attila, you don't have to protect me. I'm just going up the shore in that direction for maybe half a mile, up to where that rocky outcropping is, and I'll come right back. You'll be able to see me all the way if you want to. Nobody's going to get me, and anyway, if they did, they'd turn me loose when they got a second look."

He wrapped his arms around me. "Velvet, we haven't been alone with each other for days. I miss you. "

"I know. I miss you, too. Next week we'll be in Washington and we can be together all we want."

Bill kissed my forehead sweetly. "Huh! Is that all I'm going to get?" I complained.

He popped me on the bottom and said, "Go have a good run. When you come back we'll count all the fish I'm going to catch and pack them in the ice chest for that big fish fry tomorrow night."

Wearing my new, bright red swimsuit, I ran barefooted along the shore, chased the arcs of gentle surf as it swooshed up on the sand, bubbling and foaming around my toes, then streaming back into the sea. I was five years old again.

At the rocky outcropping I turned around to amble back toward Bill. This beach was littered with unusual shells and stones eroded into interesting shapes, and bits of weathered driftwood which had washed ashore. I stooped and studied them and dropped the most intriguing ones into my string bag. Where had these shells come traveled from? What part of the world had they seen? What tales would they tell if they could speak?

Maybe my major in college should be Beachcombing, not Political Science. I'd graduate as a Beach Bum Cum Laude.

The sun dropped low on the horizon and the surface of the sea became a brilliant, dazzling blaze of gold. Momentarily blinded by the brightness I turned away, glanced toward the dull, sandy dunes and waving sea grass, and waited for my eyes to adjust. I thought I saw a fleeting movement out of the corner of my eye. A person? Way out here? Nonsense. It was an illusion. Or a chunk of driftwood. Maybe a weed blowing from behind the dune. When my normal vision returned no one was there.

Darkness was falling. Time to hurry back along the sparkling sea to Bill, and hopefully, a mess of fish.

The exercise and peace beside the ocean had relaxed me and I felt good again, all my anxiety and fear washed away with the surf. It's my theory that quiet time beside the sea can cure any ill, and

I've always told my dad that if I ever lost my mind, not to put me in a hospital, just take me to the ocean and let me run on the shore.

It must be a pretty good theory: twenty-four hours ago I was practically crazy with fear, and now I was perfectly—well, reasonably—okay.

Chapter 51.

"Good fishing?" I called when I got close enough for Bill to hear me over the roar of the surf.

"Yes. Mackerel, sea bass and corvinas. Enough for a fish fry. How about you? Is that a sack full of shells? Are you ready to go home?"

"No, not yet. Why don't we build a fire and watch the moon come up? I saw plenty of driftwood less than fifty feet away."

"Great idea! I'll get the wood. Would you grab some of those newspapers from the trunk? There are matches in the fishing creel."

The breeze was becoming cooler. Time to throw sweatshirts over our swimsuits.

When the fire was roaring, Bill scooped a hollow in the sand where we could sit, his arms around me, and watch the blaze and the silver moonlight glittering on the black sea. We talked about our plans for the future: Bill's law practice, my college work, our marriage and careers. This seemed like the right time to bring up a subject I felt we needed to talk about.

During a pause in the conversation I said, "Can I ask you something?"

"Yes. What?"

"Remember the day you got here and I told you about our new gardener, Pablo?"

"Yes."

"It made you so furious I thought you were going to have a coronary. It showed in your tight jaw muscles and your clenched fists. Every time I've mentioned my father since then, you've gotten tense, withdrawn from me, and acted cool and aloof. I thought you liked my father, but there's obviously something that's getting in the way of our relationship."

Bill had a startled expression, as though I had unclothed him, left him naked for anyone to see.

"I don't mean to pry, but don't you think this is critical? What is it about my father that makes you so angry? It's not just concern for my safety, is it?"

Bill frowned, silent, deliberating.

I waited, worried.

"Velvet, you're right, of course. I am concerned, very concerned, about your safety, but yes, there is more to it than that.""Then talk to me. Please. I need to know."

He turned away for a moment, then faced me, laid his hands on my shoulders, and looked directly into my eyes.

"Velvet, it's difficult to say this because I care so much for you and I don't want to hurt your feelings. But, think back to that afternoon when you told us about Pablo and how frightened you were with nobody around to help you. Your words were, 'I wished Dad were here'."

"Well, I did wish that," I said, defensively.

"That's exactly the point. I want you to wish _I_ were here, not your father. I want to be the one you turn to, the one to help you. Do you know what it's like to be in love with a daddy's girl? Especially a rich daddy's girl? My boss' only child? God knows I'm not trying to take his place. I'd never do that to you. But I am trying to create a place of my own and be the one who shares your life, the first one you think of, the one you want to be with."

His words hit me hard. I'd never thought about it that way. Now it was as plain as could be. I knew, of course, that I had led a protected life surrounded with love and care. In some ways I was fairly immature and naive, but that's the way my parents brought me up. They wanted me to be modest, concerned for others, and strong. I grew up believing my mother and father were wonderful. It never occurred to me how someone else might look at it.

"Do you understand what I'm trying to say?" Bill asked softly, his hands caressing my shoulders.

"Yes. I think so. And I'm sorry. I'm so sorry. I didn't realize what I was doing."

Well, I knew now. I had some changes to make. Was this just the beginning?

Bill gently stroked my cheek with his fingers, touched his lips to mine, and looked into my eyes so deeply there was no further need for words.

Slowly, he leaned back on the sand, moonlight on his clean-cut face. He reached up and placed his hands on my shoulders to pull down and hold me close.

As I leaned over him to kiss him, I caught the glint of moonlight on metal on top of the dune. There was a rush of air close to my ear. Something brushed through my hair and hit the sand beside me with a dull thud.

"What was that?" Bill jerked to his feet.

Our attention was captured by an object stabbing the beach. We knelt to examine it.

"Don't touch it!" Bill commanded harshly. He ripped off his shirt, wrapped it around the object, and pulled it from the sand.

"A knife," I whispered.

"Yes. A diver's stiletto. Razor sharp. A four-and-a-half inch blade serrated on each side. Straight handle with a metal tip for striking."

I shuddered. All the old fears returned. "What's it all about?"

"I don't know. But someone almost killed you. Again."

Chapter 52.

"It's practically midnight," Bill said as we drove into our graveled driveway, "but all the lights inside and out are blazing. Everyone must still be awake."

He hadn't even turned off the ignition when Eric came tearing out of the house, with everyone else running behind him. Even Maria, and she should have gone home hours ago. But come to think of it, both she and my mother had always waited up for me to come home, so I shouldn't have been surprised.

Eric jerked open my door and yelled, "Where have you been? We've been worried to death!"

Bill got out of the car and walked briskly around to my door. Possessively, he reached for my hand and assisted me to the driveway. "We've been worried to death ourselves," he said grimly.

I could see the wheels turning in everyone's minds: what kind of trouble had kept us so long?

"Come inside," Sandy said. "I made coffee."

"Do you mind if I close the drapes?" Bill asked when we entered the living room to sit down.

"Let me," Jade said and hurried from window to window, pulling the heavy drapes closed.

Seated, eyes moving between Bill and me, everyone was on edge. But I felt strangely calm, not at all trembley and dry-mouthed like I had been for all those hours since the attack.

"There was another attempt on Velvet's life," Bill began. Our friends' faces registered alarm, and they leaned forward, shocked and tense.

"I'd finished fishing and Velvet came back from beachcombing. We built a driftwood fire and sat down to watch the moon come up. All of a sudden, from the top of a big sand dune, someone threw a diver's stiletto at Velvet. It hurtled right through her hair and landed, point down, in the sand a few inches away. If she hadn't leaned down at that instant, the knife would have ripped through her chest."

"That devil!" Maria screeched from the door where she was standing and listening. Almost hysterical, the tiny lady rushed to me, cupped my face in her hands, her fringed shawl cascading from her shoulders onto the floor. "You poor child. Did he hurt you? Are you all right?"

"I'm fine, dear. Don't be upset. I'm fine," I assured her and patted her back. "Did you tell the police?" she asked.

Bill answered. "We raced to the police station in Guaymas and the officer on duty phoned the chief at home. He came to the station and took our statement."

"What did he think and say?" Eric asked.

"He said a pattern was emerging and he wanted to take some men and us back to the beach to look for tracks and other clues. He rode with us, and four officers with spotlights and flashlights followed us in a police car."

"Did you find anything? Was it too dark?" Sandy asked.

"Fairly dark, yes, but the moon was full. That helped. The officers found footprints in the sand. They back-tracked about a quarter of a mile up the road and found tire tracks where someone had parked a car. The officers followed the footprints through the desert in a circuitous route, sometimes doubling back and then going on toward the beach again. They led to the big dune where we were lying in the sand."

"But you didn't hear anyone?" Eric asked.

"No, not with the surf crashing and the fire crackling. But Chief Salinas said he could tell from the footprints that the man had run all the way back to his car."

"Then what?" Sandy pressed.

"Then we all drove back to the police station and the chief talked with us."

"What did he say?" Eric asked.

"He said he can almost break this case, maybe as soon as tomorrow, but he wants Velvet to stay at home until he lets us know he's made an arrest."

"That doesn't mean all the rest of you have to stay here, though," I was quick to add. "In fact, it would make me feel better if you'd go ahead and do everything you came to San Carlos to do. It's almost your last chance, you know."

"I think you should get some sleep now, if you can, and we'll talk about it tomorrow, okay?" Sandy said and took my empty coffee cup.

Maria had stayed in the living room as one of the family. Now she stated resolutely, "I will be right here every minute. You can be sure no one will harm this child as long as I'm alive." She clearly intended that to be a very long time. Maria looked meek and fragile, but she was actually as protective and feisty as a tiger with a cub. I was very glad she was my tiger mom.

Chapter 53.

It must have been three in the morning before I finally fell asleep. I tossed and tumbled, pursued by ugly groupers and divers with stiletto knives. In dreams my arms and legs wouldn't move. It was like trying to swim through Jello.

Gradually, my nightmares faded and the ordinary sounds of the sea gently slapping the cliff penetrated my brain. My eyes creaked opened, but my body was reluctant to move. Gotta get up, I told myself. But I didn't.

I sensed the presence of someone in my room, and with nerves strung tight, I jerked my head around to see who was there.

"I'm sorry, little one," Maria said. "I didn't mean to startle you. I have been watching so that I would know when you were awake."

"Where's everybody?" I asked and sat up.

"The men are at the marina taking care of the boat. Sandy is on the cliff, painting a picture for the living room. And Jade is down at the cove taking a swim."

"Did I miss breakfast?" I was so hungry my stomach was growling. It hadn't had anything to run on but nerves since lunch yesterday.

"Everyone else has eaten. What would you like?" Maria asked. "I'll bring a tray and you can eat in bed.

I grinned. That's what Mother used to do when I was sick. Sometimes I'd just pretend and I thought I was fooling her, but last winter she laughed and told me she'd always known.

"Thanks, Maria. I'll please have three eggs, four strips of bacon, a stack of pancakes, coffee, juice and fruit."

Maria's mouth dropped open in astonishment. Then she threw back her head and laughed. "You are just like your father. Your eyes are bigger than your stomach. But I'll cook it just the same. You need more meat on your bones."

The breakfast Maria prepared was delicious but if it happened very often, my blue jeans would be destined for the Salvation Army bin. After I finished eating I relaxed in a deep bubblebath, shampooed my hair, and put on fresh white shorts and a cotton shirt.

"Good morning, Lazybones," Bill greeted me when he, Eric and Lee returned from the marina. "You look gorgeous. It does you good to sleep in."

"Thanks. You don't look so bad yourself. What's the news at the marina?"

"Everybody's talking about the attack on you. It even made the newspaper and TV this morning. Chief Salinas is asking that anyone who has seen or heard anything suspicious call him."

"I think he's going to solve this case today," Eric stated. "He'll catch that guy, whoever he is, and put him in jail, and we'll be able to enjoy our last two days in Mexico."

"That's plenty fine with me," I declared. "I want you to take happy memories back home when you leave."

"We will," Eric said. "Now let's go find our artist and see what she's painting."

"I'll go down to the cove and get Jade," Lee said. "We'll meet you on the cliff."

Thankfully, all our tension from last night dissolved in the sunlight of morning. Why is it our anxieties and fears seem worse when it's dark and we're alone? Is it man's destiny to fear the dark and look forward to the dawn?

Chapter 54.

We had barely finished eating lunch and Maria and I were clearing the kitchen table when someone pounded on the front door.

I jumped, startled, my nerves on edge again. "Are you expecting anyone?" Maria asked in concern.

"I'll go," Bill said.

We heard the heavy carved door open and close, and greetings in the entryway. At least the caller was friendly. In a moment Bill returned with the Guaymas Chief of Police. He took off his cap. "Good afternoon. I hope I'm not disturbing you."

"Sit down, Chief," Eric invited and brought another chair to the table.

"Thank you. I have good news for you." The chief smiled, his white teeth gleaming. "We have your man."

"Thank heavens!" Sandy said. Bill and Eric reached across the table and shook the chief's hand.

"How did you get him?" Bill asked.

"We were fairly sure of our fellow, but we needed a little more evidence. After the news media covered the story and our request for anyone who had seen anything suspicious to come forward, we received two phone calls that tipped us off to the motive for someone trying to kill Miss Shepard. At about the same time, the driver of a Pemex oil tanker walked into the police station and asked if we had caught the man we were looking for."

We leaned forward to hear what had happened.

"He told us he was driving north on the coast highway at about nine o'clock last night, and just south of Empalme some guy with car trouble flagged him down. The Pemex driver gave him a lift into Guaymas and dropped him at a house near the center of town."

"And then?" Bill urged.

"And then the driver took us to that house. We knocked on the door and when a man answered, the driver identified him as being the same one he'd given a ride to last night. We took the man out on the highway past Empalme and when we came to the car stalled on the side of the road, he admitted it was his. His tires had the same tread as the tracks to the Playa where you built your fire. We found white sand in the carpet, sand-covered huaraches that looked to be about the same size as the footprints on the dunes, and the empty sheath for a diver's knife. He told us somebody had stolen the knife out of his car and left the sheath. Not a very believable story.""Did you have enough evidence to arrest him?" Bill asked. "Did he give a confession?"

"We had enough to hold him for questioning, but he has not confessed; in fact, he denied any connection to you. Said he didn't know what we were talking about; however, those two phone calls we received about the case gave us information about a Texas cowboy named Matthew Armes who once worked on Senator Shepard's ranch and now lives in Guaymas. Does that name mean anything to you, Miss Shepard?"

The name did ring a bell. "Yes, I remember that man. He worked for us last fall, but he wouldn't follow orders, the foreman's or Dad's, either. Dad told the cowboy he had too short a fuse. The man got into fights with several of our other men, and one day he attacked the foreman with a pitchfork. Dad called the sheriff, but the man got away and we never heard from him again."

The chief said, "That's what our callers told us. What I think is this cowboy knew your family has a home here, and waited for a chance to get even with your father. What better way than to terrorize and then kill his only daughter?"

"Do you think he's responsible for the two murders in San Carlos, too? And the maliciousness with our boat? Or the attack on Velvet at Haystack Rock?" Bill asked.

The chief massaged the tension muscles in the back of his neck. "I personally think so, but he hasn't admitted it yet and we don't have enough evidence to charge him with those crimes. We'll get a confession, though. It's just a matter of time."

"What about all those guns and knives and dynamite in the cave in the cliff?" I asked, unable to forget how surprised and scared I was at finding them in that secluded hideaway, and the fear when Jade and I found the dead rabbit where we tied our horses.

"We checked the cave and questioned Armes. There doesn't seem to be any connection. We think whoever is living in the cave is just some American hippy who's found a warm climate and is using the cave for shelter and seclusion," the chief said. "That's not against the law."

"Is there anything you want us to do now?" Bill asked.

"Yes, there is. I need Miss Shepard to come take a look at this Armes fellow and see if she recognizes him not just as the senator's ranch hand, but also for the other times she's seen someone suspicious and to try and identify him as the diver who tried to kill her. After that, you can all feel free to go diving or skiing or anything else you want to do. We've got this guy in jail and that's where he's going to stay for a while. Maybe quite a while."

Chapter 55.

"This is our last full day south of the border," Sandy said at breakfast the next morning, "and I've hardly begun to paint all these wonderful scenes."

"Why don't we spend the day with the camera and you can paint from photographs when we get home?" Eric suggested.

"I'd like to take pictures too," Lee said, "and send them to my family in Shanghai to see what the west coast of Mexico is like." He smiled at Jade. "I want to get pictures of Jade, too." If Jade wasn't sure about Lee's feelings by now, she never would be.

"Can we water ski, too?" Jade asked.

"You bet. You can ski 'til your arms drop off and there are barnacles on your bottom," Eric assured her.

"Velvet? Bill? What do you want to do?"

"I don't want to be a wet blanket," I said hesitantly, "but I'd like to stay home alone today."

Bill looked hurt. "Why do you want to stay alone? Don't you want me to stay with you?"

"No, actually not. Today is my mother's birthday and we almost always celebrated it here. I'd just like to remember the way it used to be, and I don't think I'd be very good company on the boat. Okay?"

"Yes, sure," Bill said, but he wasn't happy about being shut out.

"Maria and I'll pack a lunch and beach towels for you," I offered. "Take the boat and go anyplace you want to and have a great time."

By the time Maria and I finished packing the lunch Sandy and Lee came into the kitchen carrying cameras and extra film. Eric grabbed the stack of towels and hauled them to the van.

Bill picked up the ice chest and asked, "You're sure you don't want me to stay? You know I want to."

"I'm sure. Shoo! Go have fun. I'm just going to stay at home and stay quiet. I'm missing my mom, and I'm kinda wrung out anyway."

Bill bent over the ice chest he was lugging, intending to kiss me goodbye. I threw my arms around his neck to let him know I really did love him and was sorry to send him away, but in doing it I accidentally knocked the cover off the ice chest. Crushed ice skittered all over the tile floor, under the table and chairs and the china cabinet, and under the refrigerator and stove. "Miss Klutz scores again," I sighed.

Bill groaned his "I'll be damned" groan, set the chest on the floor and got down on his hands and knees to help me pick up the ice. Concentrating on finding all the chips before they melted, not looking where we were going, we bumped heads under the table.

"Okay, before I put all this ice back in the chest, how about a rewarding hug from my Krazy Kisser?" he grinned.

"Fie on you. You have absolutely no appreciation for the subtleties of true love."

"Subtleties? If that was a demonstration of subtlety, I can hardly wait to see a bit of enthusiasm," he laughed and crawled from under the table. He dumped the ice into the chest, replaced the lid, and looking back, squeezed sideways out the door. "Stay cool," he laughed.

I tried unsuccessfully to give him an icy stare. "I don't know why you're packing an ice chest when you have such a heart of ice," I said. I should know. He was wearing his heart on his sleeve.

Chapter 56.

After they left, I walked listlessly into the front yard where Pablo was cleaning the fishpond and waterfall. "I'm finished, Miss, unless there's something else you want me to do."

"No, you have the yards in beautiful shape. I'm very pleased."

"I'll be going, then. Until tomorrow," he said and carried his tools to the carport storage room. I watched him put the tools away, close the door and shuffle away with a limp. It was such a relief to know he was exactly what he said he was, our gardener, and not responsible for any of the frightening things that had been happening.

"Velvet, where are you?" Maria called from the kitchen door.

"Right here. I'm coming. Do you want something?"

"No, I was just checking," she said.

"You don't need to worry any more, Maria. Everything is fine now. You heard Chief Salinas say they'd caught Matthew Armes and our problems are over."

"Yes, I heard, but I still have a bad feeling in the bottom of my soul."

I hugged the delicate little lady who meant so much to me. "I'm going to straighten my room now and spend the afternoon on the terrace. It's been a long time since I've seen our family photo album. Don't you think this is an appropriate time to look at it? I have a new book I haven't had any time to break open so I think I'll start on it, too."

"Good, and I won't disturb you. I'll set a pitcher of limeade and a glass by the chaise lounge on the terrace. If you want anything else, I'll be in the kitchen peeling shrimp," she said.

I finished cleaning my room and changed into a swimsuit so brief I only wore it at home. It didn't make any difference to me that other girls wore suits as skimpy as this at public beaches and pools, but I personally felt overexposed and under-confident in it except for solitary sunbathing.

I took the family album to the terrace and opened it to photos of my mother at the sport fishermen's dock in Guaymas where she was weighing the sailfish she'd caught one summer. Other photos showed her grilling shrimp over charcoal on the beach; diving off the cliff into the sea; and smiling aboard the boat. There were dozens of pictures of my mother and father together, and a few pictures of them with me. Those had been wonderful, happy days and I'd always remember them.

Mother had been dead for five months, but I hadn't cried at all 'til now. I had missed my mother badly, but I'd kept myself insulated in a frenzy of activities with crowds of people. Now, all at once, like a dam weakened by an over-filled lake, my grief broke and tears poured down my face. I cried 'til there weren't any tears left, then fell asleep in the sunshine.

Sometime later, I don't know how long it was, a sound, a thud, penetrated my dreams. I listened, still half asleep, but there weren't any further sounds. Maria must have dropped something in the kitchen, I decided, and drowsed off again.

Then, not understanding what was happening, I felt the keen pressure of a razor-sharp knife against my throat. I was shocked wide awake. My muscles jerked tight and I struggled to sit up.

"Stay there. Don't move! I've got you all to myself now, Jade, there's no one else around," a deep, loud voice roared in my ear.

Jade? Did he say Jade? Did this guy think I was Jade?

Terrified, I looked into the man's face only inches from mine, and the insane, burning eyes of a man I recognized. Big. Muscular. Medium-long light hair. The same hair I'd seen flowing in the current at Haystack Rock. This was the man who'd ripped away my air supply. The man who'd driven past our house and covered our gear with dust that day when we first arrived. The man on the dining terrace in the citrus grove at the hotel. And the man Jade saw in the boat when she skied at Algodones. Who was he? Why was he here?

"Don't scream. I'll slash your throat if you make a sound. There's no one to hear you, anyway, he commanded. "Do you remember the rabbit with its eyes poked out? That's only part of what I'm going to do to you."

I was paralyzed with fear. I couldn't even whisper, let alone scream. But who was this guy? Why did he call me Jade? What did he have to do with her anyway?

I closed my eyes. Be calm, I told myself. Do exactly what he says. Nothing's going to happen. He'll see I'm not Jade and go away.

But he didn't.

With a gruesome grin the demented man drew the blade of his knife across my throat and I knew this was the moment I was going to die. Horrified, I felt the skin on my throat open and blood race down my neck. My jugulars? Did he slash my jugular veins? There would be no help. I would die. For no reason at all.

But then the attack stopped as abruptly as it had started. Looking behind him, the man yanked the knife from my throat and stood unmoving for a second with sudden panic and fear in his face. Then he whirled away from me and raced toward the steps that led from the terrace down the cliff to the cove. Why? Thank God, but what scared him away?

Grasping my throat, blood running between my fingers, I turned and looked behind me, and there was Bill racing from the house. He was wild with fury, as ferocious as a maddened lion, pursuing the fleeing man.

The man with the knife still in his hand, desperate to escape Bill's wild pursuit, reached the opening in the wall and plunged the first three steps down the cliff. But suddenly he tripped on his own flopping, rubber-tire-soled sandal. Helpless to break his fall, he hurtled, screaming, down the steep, stone steps fifty feet to the boulders below.

My throat bleeding, and air rasping in my throat, I staggered to the terrace wall and looked down at the cove. Bill, winded and shaking, was already leaning over it, staring at the broken, bloodied body sprawled on the jagged rocks beside the aqua sea.

His face white and tense, Bill turned away from the sickening sight, and for the first time since the attack he looked at me.

"Velvet, Velvet, what did he do to you?" He picked me up and carried me to the chaise lounge. "Lie down. Don't move."

He tore off his shirt and wrapped it around my throat, pressing hard against the slash. When there finally seemed to be less bleeding he blotted the wound and carefully examined it.

"Velvet, he only broke the skin. The cuts aren't deep and he missed the arteries. You're going to be all right."

"What happened?" I managed to ask. "Who was that? Why did he knife me? He wasn't even after me. He was after Jade."

All at once I remembered that I hadn't been at home alone. I tried to jump up, but Bill firmly pushed me back down.

"Where's Maria? Is Maria all right?"

"Shh. Stay quiet. Maria's in the kitchen with Lee."

"Why with Lee? What's...?"

"Just lie still. We don't want this bleeding to start again. Everything's going to be all right. The guy must have slipped into the kitchen when Maria had her back to the door. She was sitting at the table peeling shrimp when he hit her head from the back and knocked her out, but she's conscious now and probably doesn't have anything worse than a concussion and a bad scare. She's already trying to come see about you but Lee is making her stay down until her dizziness goes away."

"What about Sandy and Eric and Jade?" I whispered, afraid for them, too.

"They're on the way. They don't know anything's happened. They've been buttoning down the boat.""What brought you and Lee back ahead of them? How did you happen to get here when you did?"

"When we got back to the marina we tied up at the dock and Lee walked up to the store to buy some peanuts. While he was there, your watchdog gardener, Pablo, walked in. He said something nutty like, 'It will happen today and I cannot stop it.' Lee, in his inscrutable, ancient Oriental wisdom, was so spooked he came running back to the boat and persuaded me we should come check on you. So here we are."

At that moment the kitchen door slammed. We heard Jade scream and voices shouting in the kitchen. Eric, Penny and Jade came running out of the house. They stopped cold in front of Bill, his red, bloody shirt around my neck.

"Velvet, what....?"

Obviously shaken but nevertheless calm, Bill said, "There's a body at the foot of the cliff. Can you find a phone and call the police?"

They sprinted to the wall and leaned over it to look at the body sprawled grotesquely over the boulders. They gasped so loudly we could hear them from across the terrace. It sounded like a gasp of horror, but also one of recognition.

"How can it be?" Jade whispered. "Why?" She began shaking violently and tears shimmered in her eyes.

Lee wrapped his arms around her, rubbed her shoulders and rocked her back and forth until she stopped trembling and sobbing.

"Eric, was that someone you knew? Bill asked, puzzled.

"That was someone we knew," Eric said, his voice filled with terrible regret.

Chapter 57.

"No, I don't want to go to the hospital," I objected. The paramedics frowned.

"I'll be perfectly all right here at home. What about Maria?"

"She had a bad scare and a hard blow to her head, but she's going to be fine. All she needs is a sedative to settle her nerves, and a good night's sleep," one of the medical men said. "And so do you, but you also have superficial cuts on your throat. We don't think you'll have any more bleeding, but we would like to keep you under observation for twenty-four hours."

"No, it's kind of you to want to watch me, but I can be observed at home just as well."

"If that's what you want, all right, but call us if you do have any more bleeding. And now we'll help the police bring the body up the steps and get back to town."

The Chief of Police supervised while his men put the broken, bloody dead man into a body bag. They strapped it to a litter and carried it up the steep cliff. We watched their muscles strain and heard their heavy breathing when they stopped at each landing to catch their wind.

"Did you say the man called you Jade?" the chief asked after the ambulance and most of the officers drove away. "Why would he know Jade? How did he know she was here? Who is the man?"

Lee spoke up. "His name is Scott Carter. He went to high school in Denver with Jade. Last summer he joined a team of runners Jade was in and went to China with the group. I met them in Shanghai as one of their guides. When we were in the Summer Palace in Beijing, Scott went berserk and attacked Jade for no reason. She somehow managed to break away from him and run out an exit to safety."

"Was the man arrested?" the chief asked.

"No, he caught the first flight to Hawaii and none of us ever saw him again."

Lee went on to relay the information Jade's father had learned about Scott: the childhood with a drunken father who regularly humiliated him and beat him, and his small, dark-haired, meek mother who let it happen time and again. He described the neighbors' pets, their throats slashed and their eyes punctured; and, the women Scott had brutalized.

"I think this is a classic case of someone whose mind is warped. He keeps trying to kill his own mother, but can't distinguish between one small, dark-haired woman and another," the chief speculated. "I'm going to bet he murdered the two girls in San Carlos, and that we'll learn of others when this thing hits the wires. I think you girls are very lucky to be alive."

I shuddered. I thought so, too. It made me wonder: what was the mathematical probability in the history of mankind that each of the tiny, insignificant circumstances in all our lives could bring us together at this single moment in this single place? I figured it was so minuscule that it couldn't happen at all.

But it had.

Bill said to the chief, "Do you think the guy somehow found out Jade would be here and waited for her?

The chief thought about it. "I don't know. Maybe he just happened to come here, drifting from one country to another. He might have stumbled on to the cave by chance and decided to make it his home base while he looked around."

Bill added to the speculation, "And while he was looking around he discovered a small, dark-haired American woman. His twisted mind thought it was his mother and he bashed in her head and threw her into the sea to punish her for never rescuing him from his father. You found her when the tide carried her into the marina."

Eric said, "A few weeks later he saw his 'mother' again and he killed her, too, but that didn't make sense even in his mind and it made him more cautious in his mixed-up way."

"I think it was pure chance that he drove past this house while both Jade and Velvet were in the carport, and he came back around for a second look. I'm also going to say he watched them every place they went for the next three weeks, trying to sort out which one was really his mother," Bill said.

I added, "So he watched us ride horses to the palm trees and climb up the mountain, and when we discovered his weapons in the cave he knew he had to scare us so bad we'd stay away. He didn't know yet which one of us to kill and needed more time to spy on us. He probably watched us dive every day, and I know he was the man in the shadows when we had dinner in the citrus grove at the hotel."

Jade said, "And the day I was skiing at Algodones, that was him watching from the boat. When he slashed his throat with his hand he was really warning me that was what he was going to do to me."

Bill unraveled the mystery some more. "He must have gotten confused about which one he was going to kill and decided to create a boat accident at sea. He stole the life jackets and flares and drained out so much gas we would only be able to reach the island but wouldn't get back again. And then the storm came up and that made it even worse."

"What about the morning he ripped away my air supply?" I asked.

Lee answered, "Didn't you and Jade trade wetsuits that day? Wasn't it the only time? He undoubtedly knew by then that Jade's suit and mask were pink, so that's the one he went after. If he ever realized he was wrong, it was too late. He had to get away."

Bill said, "Then today he saw just one of these dark-haired women board the boat for a day of skiing and just naturally assumed it was Velvet because it's her boat. That's when he decided Jade would be alone and he could do away with her. But, he didn't reckon on Pablo's so-called psychic powers or Lee believing in them. If Lee hadn't listened to that batty old man, Velvet would be dead now."

We sat in silence, vacantly looking at our hands in our laps, trying to accept the whole crazy thing.

The chief broke the silence. "And I was wrong about Matthew Armes, your ranch hand. It was Carter, not Armes, who tailed you to the Playa west of Empalme and threw the knife at you. Armes was mad at the senator, all right, but he didn't commit any crimes. He just happened to be in the wrong place at the wrong time. Like you," he said pointedly to Jade and me.

"Is it over now?" I asked. "Is it all over?"

"It is for now," the chief said. "I want to express my regret that you had these problems, and I hope they won't ruin your impression of Mexico. Come back soon and do some more diving. 'Til then, goodbye."

The chief shook our hands and marched briskly out the door. For a few moments we each were lost in our own thoughts.

"What are we going to tell Dad?" I asked, worried. "Sooner or later he's going to hear about it, and he ought to hear it from us before then."

"How about telling him you did exactly what he wanted you to do? Tell him you had a vacation you'll never forget," Eric suggested.

"Oh, Eric, you know that'll never fly."

Bill said, "Try this suggestion. Since this will be our last night in Mexico, and it might be years before Lee and Jade get to China again for any Beijing duck fajitas, why don't we take them to the cantina on the beach for dinner later tonight after we've gotten over some of this shock? We can ask the cook if he'll make duck fajitas and sharkfin soup. Later, we can listen to the guitarist sing. Lee, Jade, what do you say?"

"Great idea! Glad you thought of it," Lee said. "But to tell you the truth, I'd rather have some of those fresh crab enchiladas Maria introduced me to. It'll be tough to find any when I get back to China. So if that's okay with you, let's go. I'm buying!"

El fin, amigo.
¡Hasta luego!